M000310033

To Ann,

"... we spend our years as a tale that is told."
Ps. 90:9

When the tale is told,
And your story we behold;
May we all rejoice,
During Story Time in Heaven!

Warm Regards,
M. V. Brum

Story Time in Heaven

Book One

Dreams, Choices, and Covenants of Love

G. T. Froese

ISBN 978-1-64458-023-3 (hardcover)
ISBN 978-1-64458-022-6 (digital)

Copyright © 2018 by G. T. Froese

All rights reserved. No part of this publication may be reproduced, distributed, or transmitted in any form or by any means, including photocopying, recording, or other electronic or mechanical methods without the prior written permission of the publisher. For permission requests, solicit the publisher via the address below.

Christian Faith Publishing, Inc.
832 Park Avenue
Meadville, PA 16335
www.christianfaithpublishing.com

Printed in the United States of America

Dedication

This book is dedicated to the glory of God, who filled my heart with great joy and inspiration each day as I was writing these words and in whose presence is my greatest delight! It is our heavenly family's story, dedicated to give Glory and Praise to the Father of Love and to His Son, Jesus Christ our Lord.

It is also dedicated to my wonderful partner in life, my wife Brenda, who was with me every day giving encouragement and praying for the Lord's guidance. She was the first one to read every word. Her support and invaluable advice helped me produce an improved work, well above what I could have achieved on my own.

A special acknowledgement to my Literary Agent, Marie Lewis. Your response after a first read of the storyline and before I had written a word; was beyond expectations! These supportive words were so encouraging and confirmed my resolve to begin this work. Thank you, Marie!

To God be the Glory!

Contents

Introduction

This is an imaginary journey to a very real place. Since childhood, I have heard stories of this place. Many of my family members are now there; none have ever returned. Much has been written in the scriptures concerning heaven. This imaginary narrative is based on my love for the accounts of the biblical writers. It is also based upon a lifetime spent in studying the scriptures.

The adventures contained within these pages are my personal dreams and thoughts concerning heaven and its citizens. I have never been there, except in my imagination. We are told, however, that it is the eternal dwelling place and the reward for all who loved God and received the sacrifice of His Son while living here upon earth. The scriptures declare that "Eye hath not seen, nor ear heard, neither have entered into the heart of man, the things which God hath prepared for them that love him. But God hath revealed them unto us by his Spirit" (1 Cor. 2:9–10, KJV).

My purpose is writing this imaginary story is:

- To share eternal truths within each inventive saga.
- To use allegory and imaginative storytelling to teach eternal laws and principles.
- To share the story of the ages (the story of God's love) in and through the lives of others.
- To share what I personally believe to be God's purpose and method in the creation of man and this universe.
- To inspire faith and trust in God, our loving heavenly Father, and in His Son Jesus Christ, our Lord!

I invite you to travel with me in the spirit of your imagination to *Story Time in Heaven.*

1

Heavenly Realities

There is a place outside of time,
There is a dimension beyond the realm of space,
A place where a family has gathered
And stories are told of amazing grace.

Let me take you there. Open your mind and your imagination as we embark on an exhilarating journey to this magnificent place. The journey cannot be done with your body because our bodies are limited to time and space. No spaceship or starship can carry you there. If you could travel at the speed of light, approach would still be impossible. Your transport must occur in your mind and in your heart. As you leave the confines of this earth, you soar in the spirit out of this atmosphere with its limitations and into the heavens and beyond.

You are primarily a spirit. You have a soul, but you live in a body only adapted to this earth. Our earthly bodies are not equipped for the expedition we are about to take. It is an adventure to a very unique and real place. Our destination is a place far more real than anything you have ever known! So let's leave this earthy sphere; journey through the vast universe; and, in the spirit, pass beyond the moon, beyond the sun, beyond the galaxy, and beyond the depths of space, translated into the ever- present eternity of God's world. Once outside of time and space, as we enter the limitless realm of eternity, we begin to appreciate how minute, how very small the Earth and universe appears in comparison! We are like a babe that just left the womb. A door has opened to a much larger life! All that is behind us now, all that we have known before has dimmed. Our past is released as we allow the light of new, eternal realities to unfold.

On earth, our bodies appear. They bloom. They are gone. In this eternal place, it is one glorious and forever day. We have slipped out of our earth suit, our physical body, just like a hand slipping free from a glove. Though the body, this earthly attachment is left far behind, we still see, we still hear, we still feel, and we still know!

Astonishment! Absolute awe! We are captivated! We seem to have an inability to form words, that would adequately express the glory and love we now feel! *Love* envelops us as we enter this place called heaven. Many who have experienced this journey before tried to convey their responses, yet no one can fully express in earthly words the vision we now behold. We find ourselves in a place without beginning or ending. Before the moon could reflect the sun's brilliant light upon the darkness of the Earth before the stars sang together or the sun began to shine. Yes, before the universe even existed. Here in heaven, there was *love*.

The expanse of this city called heaven is magnificent!! Mansions of every style and design line the streets, matching the hearts and desires of those who dwell within. Streets glisten in beauty as they are paved with rich, fine gold. Unique, park-like green areas adorn the city. They appear to bear similarity to meadows on earth, yet inexplicably different. Trees, flowers, colors, and heavenly aromas fill these spaces. We watch as people are running toward one another and embracing! They are radiant with smiles of joy! We seem to somehow know that in these parks, new arrivals are greeted by family and friends. Yes, they are greeted by those they had known and loved on earth. Millions of people fill this metropolis, much larger than any city on earth. People from all ages, time, races, and languages inhabit this unique place. They are the ones who believed in the God of heaven and worshipped Him from their hearts while on earth. These citizens of heaven all planned ahead and set their hearts on this celestial city. They stored treasures in the place where their hearts dwelt. Their treasures will remain forever, never to be lost or stolen. What a surprising group they are! Why, you ask? It is because we sense through their interactions that there is no competition, no anger, and no hate, only love and acceptance of each other. Earthly desires and anxieties have melted away, dissolved into heavenly realities! Their joy can be seen. Their love can be felt. Both can communicate with the other in a language of the spirit, the language of heaven. Earthly language is not needed in this realm of the spirit. No matter in what age they lived while on earth or what language they spoke, everyone knows each other.

Though we can see, hear, smell, feel, learn, and know; at this time, we cannot communicate with this heavenly family. We may only observe as we experience this celestial vision. Focusing our view on the inhabitants of heaven, we begin to recognize individuals we have known at one time on earth. Perhaps, like me, you see a parent, a pastor, a teacher, or a friend in your vision. Our hearts are comforted and rejoice as we see their delight and their joy! No one is sad; no one is sick; and no one is laden with cares, hurts, or disabilities. All the negative experiences on earth are passed away in the newness of light and life in heaven! Everyone is in perfect health! All tears or sorrows have been wiped away in this amazing habitation of love! Friends and family recognize and remember each other. They share a love and an understanding that washes away all fears. Truth and love wins the day forever. Perfect love truly casts away all their fears.

As we are observing their interactions and greetings of love, a call is heard, a request is made. The sound was like that of a trumpet, but it was not a clarion call to war or an alarming wake-up call. It rang out with a pleasant sound, a sweet melodic call. At the very same moment, there must have been some sort of message on a deeper level, a proclamation in the spirit. A broadcast, it seems, from the center of the city. This inner communication of the spirit is received simultaneously by everyone as a smile spread across their faces. The call is from the Father, the source of all light. His presence is what energizes and empowers this place. With no hesitation or delay, they enthusiastically respond to the summons of their Father. It is a request for all God's children to meet Him at the throne!

We begin to move with the multitudes as they make their way toward the center of this heavenly city. Everyone is singing, dancing and rejoicing with smiles and shouts of joy as they head along the way. The music has such incredible beauty! There is a perfect blending of harmony as only family can attain. Joyful, exuberant praise seems to fill the entire atmosphere! Instruments join in with symphonic sound as heaven's citizens declare the glory of the Father's love. Down streets of gold we go where incredible mansions are lining either side. What an amazing procession, a parade of praise moves along every street and merges together as we approach the mighty temple of God! Before us appears what seems to be like a sea unlike anything we had ever seen before! It is clear like glass or crystal, forming a floor beneath the feet of heaven's citizens as they enter into the throne room of God. The crystal sea is the floor of a stadium so vast that its size can contain heaven's citizens from all ages past! Everyone finds their place easily. What is truly fascinating to observe and surprises me completely is that somehow everyone in heaven's grandstand has a perfect and unobstructed view. All feel an equal closeness to the center of the scene! This stadium in heaven gives full view of God's throne, which appears to be suspended in the center. This is the throne room, the center and source of all power and all grace. It is here where our Father God, the Creator of life, the One whose presence fills all things resides and reigns supreme! In His presence, we feel so deeply His very essence, which is *love*.

As we view the scene before us, we understand how impossible it is to describe. There are colors so brilliant and pure. All the colors of the spectrum—scarlet, emerald, gold, blue, and white—are streaming light. Together they form a rainbow that encircles this magnificent throne. There is no darkness or shadows at all! We see only shimmering, glowing light and the breathtaking rainbow of color. Every component of light, a multitude of shades, is refracted into its unique wavelengths as band upon band of varying hues glistens and glows. Never has such brilliant variation of light and color been seen on earth! It is as though light itself trembles in the presence of the Father of lights.

On the throne sits the Father, the Creator of life, also referred to as the Ancient of Days. This presence on the throne seems to pulsate, vibrate, and glow with a brightness and power never seen by mortal man! Love flows in electric currents of light. We all tremble in its brilliance and life. We cannot see His face, however, we can feel His love, His power, and His life. Though the vast number of his family can't be counted by any man, the Father knows each one. This visible connection is apparent and so real! Love flows like a river, refreshing and deep. It satisfies every longing that men could ever seek. The beauty and fellowship of this family is glorious to behold!

Before his throne are two distinct objects: a beautiful, rectangular golden, chest and a golden vase emitting a pleasant aroma before the throne. This golden chest or vessel seems so important as angels are constantly hovering just above it. Cherubim and seraphim, winged beings of great beauty, seem to hover near it. These angels do not resemble the little cherubs as depicted on earth, but they are powerful, majestic beings in the presence of Almighty God. This golden container, we know instinctively, bears within something of great importance as it is directly in front of God's throne. We know its contents hold enormous significance to the entire family of God. We will learn much more about this intriguing chest as we hear the family story; yet something about it burns within us to core of our hearts as our attention is drawn to a glistening scarlet liquid overflowing down its sides. The second object is a vessel that contains a precious ointment, aromatic and pleasing to the senses. It draws the Father's attention and calls to His heart. We will learn more about this vessel also as the adventure continues and the story unfolds. Above the throne of the Father in this vast stadium, legions of angels are all assembled like great guardians and servants. They are present to serve the Father and His family. Each has their individual purpose and place in the Father's plan. Each has unique traits and powers bestowed by the God of love. Angels and archangels are present, leaders in the armies of heaven! Some angels serve as messengers, we see among them one called Gabriel. Others are mighty warriors like Michael, a powerful angel who is leading an army of these glorious beings. These are not humans who have been rewarded for doing good works on earth. They are created beings made distinct and unique by the God who inhabits eternity. They are not the children of God, but are servants and warriors for the Father God and His family. They all declare in unison the glory and majesty of God. They are also worshippers of the God of heaven! Continually they are singing, "Holy, holy, holy is the Lord!" Angels' songs are unique in their beauty as they fill heaven's stadium with their praise.

At the right hand of the Father is a throne in glory like unto His own. Seated on this throne of heaven is the mighty Son of God! Instantly, our spirits sincerely acknowledge the truth that is known within our hearts. His face is filled with love as He sees and connects with each one before Him. On His hands, feet, and side are scars that shine forth with brilliant light and intense love! We notice long golden bands on his back containing beautiful jewels. These jewels emit unequaled healing power. From what were once scars and are now precious jewels, power flows in a magnificent current of love, bringing healing and restoration to all that it touches. What power, what incredible beauty, and what amazing love! A golden crown is upon His head and a scepter in his hand. He is declared the King of kings and Lord of lords, by all the assembled angels in heaven's grandstand.

Suddenly, all the family gathered at the summons of the Father begin singing the song of redemption. The angels are now hushed in reverence and awe as God's children sing a song that the angels are unable to sing. It is the song of the Father's Love and the story of His Son. It is the family's story of God's great grace and love! Our attention is now directed to twenty-four thrones encircling the central thrones. Upon each throne, a figure clothed in pure white robes is seated. They are adorned with a golden crown upon their head. These impressive individuals have the bearing of mature, strong leaders who have conquered many foes. They have been given a place of honor and a place of authority by the ruler of all things. Their thrones all face toward the center, beholding the Father and the Son. They gaze with adoration and respect, bow their heads, and cast down their crowns. They then kneel before their Maker. Each elder places their crown beneath the feet of the Father and His glorious Son.

Victorious yet unworthy to receive the praise of men, they honor only Him who sits upon the throne! They join with the heavenly voices singing to the glory of God! The angel choirs sing as heaven's orchestra plays. Once earthly voices, now heaven's citizens, all join in a chorus of praise to the Father of love.

We could sit here forever, basking in the beauty of sight and sound. We could forever embrace the feeling of love and joy that engulfs us in this moment. We could experience unending delight in the majesty of this heavenly vision, but we are all summoned to the throne room for a reason, and the story must be told.

2

The Father's Dream

We've been summoned to hear a story,
And the story *must be told.*
It is the heavenly family's story
Of earth's beginnings in days of old.

As the Father begins to speak, all other voices cease. The Father's voice is powerful. His words send forth flashes like lightning and followed with peals of resounding thunder, reaching every ear in heaven's grandstand. The Shekinah glory of God surrounds Him like fire, causing all to tremble in awe! Yet in this auspicious moment, we somehow experience delight in the awesome warmth of his love! We are consumed, enveloped, and embraced by the glory of His presence! His voice is deep, powerful, vibrant, and electric. The gentleness and care of our heavenly Father is perceived in each word. He shares from His overflowing heart of *love*.

When the Father speaks...all others are silent. Every living being in heaven's grandstand is quieted, hushed in absolute respect and in deep abiding love. When the Father speaks, no word or confirmation is needed. We *know* that in this place, this throne room of eternity, His power is unrivaled! His knowledge is without limit. He alone is the fountain of truth. In His glorious presence, we find no need to question, no need for dispute. Here in heaven, truth is not debated but revealed. The veracity of His words are absolutely, apparent. The fear of the Lord is truly the beginning of wisdom. Our

Father opens His heart and we hear His gracious words. The Word of God, once received, is acknowledged and embraced by all. How our hearts burn within us at the very sound of His voice. Though our glorious heavenly Father speaks to a multitude, it is as though every word proclaimed is directed individually. God's words fly like an arrow straight to each heart. Our Father's voice is known in our hearts, witnessed by His Spirit. Now for the very first time, His Word is finally heard with our ears. All that He shares is eternally true! The Father's desire, His reason for bringing heaven's citizens to the throne room, is to recount some of the great episodes and events in our heavenly family's history. The accounts will be filled with origins, failures, new beginnings, great battles, and great victories as He and many others will relate their experiences. Though for generations on earth, family stories have been told around campfires, at family gatherings, and by parents with small children on their knees. Our heavenly family's story is richer by far! Get ready for wondrous adventure, and for the greatest stories ever told.

If you would know truth, if you would know love, listen closely. If you desire faith and desire success or victory, listen closely with an open heart. It is story time in heaven. The Father is sharing with His family. They are rejoicing in the glory of His grace! What could be more exciting to hear? As the heavenly story begins, the Father states, "We will begin with origins, beginnings, and eternity past." Our Father God enlightens us initially about His purpose and desire. In the depths of eternity in His eternal abode outside of time, beyond the dimension of space He alone had always existed. In His very essence, He is *love*! Before the universe came into being before time had ever begun, God reveals He had a dream, a plan. His heart overflowed with love. He desired to bring forth children to express His glory and to share His Love. He desired children in His likeness, offspring with His love, and descendants who would follow and embrace His wondrous plan. The heavenly Father's endgame, His goal and the dream in His heart was to display His great love and the riches of His grace. God desired to showcase throughout the ages to come; His children redeemed, victorious, and reflecting His *love*. This revelation displayed in His children will express the Father's kindness, grace, and love throughout the ceaseless ages, secured and transferred through Jesus Christ, His Son!

In the beginning, our Father states simply that there was only He, God the Father, the Great I Am. In the beginning, He also shares there was the Word, His Son, our Lord. In the beginning was the Holy Spirit of God. Perfect in unity, perfect in power, perfect in love. The Triune God, self-existent, all knowing and all powerful. He affirms that no one else assembled in this vast expanse of heaven's throne room even existed at the start. There was no earth or universe. There were no angels. Mankind was nonexistent. God alone contained life and inhabited eternity. He was complete in himself, needing nothing. Our heavenly Father declares that He is self-existent and self-sustaining. However, He reveals Himself as Father, Son, and Holy Spirit. In His very essence, He always was and is *love*.

Those of us who are now observing this glorious heavenly vision must be reminded that on earth, the place of our temporary residence, scientists and educators postulate and pontificate about things they do not know and haven't seen. Each person approaches the subject of origins from their own unique bias and beliefs. Their ideas change over time. Their theories come and go. God alone remains steadfast. This we *know* as we are caught up in His presence and His glory!

Before time,
Before this universe began,
Who or what?
Inquisitive minds have sought to know
The origin of life
The source of knowledge.

Longing hearts have desired to feel
The meaning of love.

A tiny speck of dust we are
In the vastness of this universe.
We appear, we bloom, and we are gone.
So small, so insignificant

Yet so unique!
We feel, we communicate,
We see,
Yet we understand so little.

We long to know
Who, how, and why.

These are the answers our Father will now share. He is the only one who was actually there! As we listen to the Father's story, we will find such great insight. He reveals that the eternal plan, the vision; was contained as a seed within His own heart. He alone created the universe. Mankind postulates about the big bang theory, a gigantic explosion—or perhaps just a sudden expansion—was its origin. They propose that something of sub-atomic size contained such dense power that when released at some point in the distant past, our gigantic universe was formed. They postulate that it happened on its own. They have no idea really, no clear ability to measure if it is true. In reality, it is as a shot in the dark. Yet to those with open eyes and ears, the truth is revealed in the light of God's Words!

Our heavenly Father speaks not in postulation or theory, but in *fact*, in revelation knowledge! In truth, God's master plan existed in His heart before it ever appeared. What was in His heart, invisible to all others for none of them even existed at that time, was a dream, a complete plan from beginning to the end. The concentrated power that scientists speculate about was in truth and substance just the dream within God's heart. His *dream* was the seed of all we see today. What the Father desired in His heart, He released through Words alone! What was in His heart, His mouth spoke, and creative power was released. His divine creative plan was released in simple words. These life-filled creative words generated a dynamic explosion of intense power. As this power was released into the empty void of eternity, miracles began! Instantly, worlds were formed out of nothing it seems. Nothing but the plan, of the heavenly Father's loving heart and the power God infused within His words. *As within an acorn is a mighty oak tree. God's words are seeds of all that eventually will be!*

The Father spoke light into darkness and the darkness was compelled to flee! "Let there be light," the Father said, and immediately light appeared! Words declared by God are alive and full of power! Our Father reminds us that words declared by His children have great power as well. *Words are pregnant with the power to produce what they proclaim!* From His throne, our Father shares to the assembled saints and angels in attendance about the days of creation and the works of His hands. The heavens and earth were created. What beauty they display! The heavens were created to declare His majestic greatness, power, and glory! As the Father describes the creation of the universe, the heavens and the earth, a visualization of all He speaks is seen as in a motion picture in the vastness of heaven's grandstand. In three-dimensional imagery we seem to view with our eyes what we hear with our ears! What a magnificent display of beauty and power we are beholding!

The earth was designed to show His creative and detailed handiwork. Each day creation speaks and every night shows forth its knowledge to all who truly seek. In every language, His voice is heard through the universe that he made. The design of each part of this vast master plan reveals the truth of our great Creator. All throughout the earth and universe, we see evidence of the master plan of the Creator and of His unique, intelligent design. All things are interdependent; all things must work in sync. All things are based on laws and are maintained, upheld, and sustained by the power of His Words! The Father goes on to enlighten us with clarity and force that in six days, He did it all. How amazing is that! Such beauty out of nothing, flinging stars into space, creating a universe so massively large, giving emphasis to his majestic and mighty power. The farther we see, the greater He appears; to those with open minds and hearts that will believe.

When you increase the visual power of the telescope that you construct, when you expand and increase the depths of the universe that man may see, you only augment, heighten, and extend the glory of God that is revealed. Suppositions are so often proven wrong for those who refuse to believe. What man would say takes millions of years took Almighty God just a day. We see before us on the heavenly visual screen a display of depth and beauty beyond what any man has ever seen. Neither the Hubble telescope nor the Chandra X-ray Observatory has ever viewed even a portion of the universe we see! Planetary systems, star systems, and billions of galaxies with millions of stars each! We see such unique, individual beauty in the variety and composition. The shapes, colors, brilliance, and power is absolutely breathtaking! It is as though we are seeing it happen before us! What was a black nothingness is now filling with beauty, depth, and dimension beyond our imagination. We are witnessing the birth of the universe before our very eyes! It all began with just a word of the Almighty!

His fingerprint is evidence of the Father's genius as no two are exactly alike, whether snowflake, man, or beast. We are here by creative genius, not an accident or a mistake. Build a microscope more powerful to magnify and enlarge the view of God's creation, make the minute particles of life more visible, and all you will see speaks even more clearly of His unique and creative design. The heavenly Father goes on to expound about His incredible joy as those six days took shape. His creative plan was coming to fruition. What a masterpiece, what artistic beauty, what detail of design! From the universe to the earth, to the lands, and to the sea. Next, life was brought forth. The seas teemed with innumerable creatures of every size. No aquarium on earth has ever given us the view we now behold. As we seem to enter in to the sea, we observe schools of fish of every shape and variety. It is as though the Father shows us on the heavenly screen under a magnifying glass the simplest forms of life and then expands our view larger and larger as the variety of fish move about us in grace and beauty. He then takes us upon land and we watch as it is filled with amazing variety of shapes and colors of plant life and then animal life! Each piece of the puzzle, from the simplest of organisms to the most advanced, was lovingly and intricately designed. This master plan was formulated in the mind and heart of God so that all things work together in perfect harmony, support, and interdependent design! The closer you look, the more clearly you behold its distinctive beauty. As He examined His work, the Father declared, "It was good!" Now the Father expounds one final touch is needed, the very purpose in it all.

On the sixth day of creation, there was agreement. The Father, Son, and Spirit, the Great I Am, the Triune God said, "Let us make man in our image. Let us make man in our likeness." Regarding all the previous days of creation, in all that God had made, He used words alone. In the final act of creation, the creation of man, the Father went beyond even words and took special care of the creation process. The Father came down from heaven to this newly formed universe and to this earth! The great sculptor of the universe made clay out of the dust of the earth. God formed an amazing body for man. This very first man was sculpted, designed, formed, and shaped in detail by the hand of the Almighty God. His body was created to interact with the world and dwell in it. It would be strengthened by the sun above and nourished by the seeds, nuts, fruits, and plants that the Father created. This body would be refreshed and sustained as well by the cool, clear waters of his home. Through the air that he breathes, man's body would be enhanced and filled with the interactive life-flow from this planet. Truly God created man a body built uniquely for this earth. Once the image was formed, once man was designed, God bent down beside him. In an act of miraculous power and love, the Father declares, "I breathed my life into this body and I created a son!"

The hushed multitudes of heaven could be silent no longer! Shouts of praise now ring forth, "Hallelujah to our God!" With great thankfulness, His children sing, "Glory to God! Praise to our heavenly Father!" The vast stadium of heaven, filled with millions of strong voices, pulsates with praise as they all rise to their feet, in standing ovation for the greatness and glory of the Father they so love!

Though we are but observers of this heavenly scene, we tremble with excitement and delight for we are hearing the true story of our birth from the Father we so love!

3

Dust Comes to Life

From dust I was formed,
From dust I was made.
When I opened my eyes,
I beheld the face of God!

The rejoicing multitude is gently calmed by the loving Father's voice. There is so much still to share. The story continues to unfold. Heaven's grandstands are now hushed as the Father directs our attention to another speaker standing among the crowd. "Who can he be?" we wonder. But we soon shall know. He will continue to tell the family history, the Story of the Ages . . . and of a Father's love.

The speaker says, "When I opened my eyes, I saw the face of God! No man had lived before me for I was uniquely born by the breath of Almighty God! As His breath flowed into my nostrils, it began to course through the dust. Dust turned into tissue, organs, muscles, bones, nerves, and blood vessels. My heart began beating and my lungs were filled with the life and breath of God! A spirit was birthed, a soul was created, and a body fashioned all at one time! Truly, I was fearfully and wonderfully made! When I opened my eyes for the very first time, I not only beheld the face of God, but I looked into my Father's eyes and I saw my best friend!" Adam continued, "The Father lifted me up from the dust. He planted my feet on the ground. He gave me His life and His love and called me His son. He gave me power to reign and rule in dominion over this world. He charged me with responsibility over the world that He made. We talked as we walked together. My Father and I enjoyed our times of fellowship. We enjoy meeting daily in the cool of the evening. Together we surveyed all the handiwork that the Father's words created. Such beauty was beyond incredible! Trees of every variety formed a forest of green interspersed with meadows of lush grass and delicate flowers. Color was everywhere on winged birds and brightly-colored flowers of intricate design. He placed me in a garden called Eden beside still waters and in green pastures of pleasure. The aroma of this place was divine. All of this the Father created with the power of His words!"

Adam shared that the Father directed him to "name everything." The fish and the fowl, the insects and beasts, and every tree and plant in the garden. What he named them, they were called by heaven and on earth. Adam studied their unique characteristics. A name was given that identified their traits and design. All the animals responded to the instructions Adam gave because the Father delegated that authority to him. He made him ruler and gave him dominion and authority over all the fish of the sea, the fowl of the air, and every living thing that moved on this earth. Animals were at peace with one another. The lion would lay down with the lamb and both were safe and satisfied. Creatures large and small, from dinosaurs to deer, all dined on the lush vegetation. They ate herbs and seeds and fruit of every kind.

There was peace in this place, safety, and the sweet aroma of love. Everything was in harmony, everything was in sync. There is no fear, no stress, and no strain. With delegated authority, there is also delegated responsibility and accountability. One amazing gift, a very unique ability, was bestowed upon Adam by his Father. This gift was not given to any other creature upon this earth, only to Adam. He was given the power to choose. This power allowed Adam to use his own mind, will, and emotions to creatively direct his responsibilities in this life. The master plan, the big picture was delegated by his Father, but the direction within boundaries was delegated to Adam. He had the ability and authority to make many decisions about the area he had control over. This amazing power gave Adam management, mastery, and authority over his world and over his own destiny in many ways. Within this power was a great potential for both good and evil. He was not created a robot, but a son. As God directed Adam to be the ruler on earth, Adam informs us that he was given clear instructions concerning one uncommon and unique tree. He was given permission to eat the fruit of every tree except for this one tree that stood in the middle of the garden. This tree—whose fruit would be deadly—was called the tree of the knowledge of good and evil. Adam understood the Father's instructions clearly and the consequence that he would die if he ate this poisonous fruit. During the beginnings in the garden as he discharged his responsibilities, he wisely abstained from sampling its fruit just as directed.

During those early days, the Father watched over His son. He relays to us that He was pleased with the way Adam managed the garden and interacted with the earth and animals. He enjoyed observing how he would responded to the other creatures that He made. Adam was using his delegated power and authority well. However, the heavenly Father knew His son needed a partner, a helper, another friend to walk beside him in this life. No other creature could satisfy his needs. In the spirit, Adam had perfect fellowship with the Creator of life. The connection needed was there. In his body, Adam received strength and sustenance from the earth, through its fruit, water, and air. He, and all other life, also received nutrients from the sun's energizing rays. The connection so needed was also there. But in his soul, something was missing completely! Adam was created a three-fold being in the image of our heavenly Father. He was a spirit by the breath of the Father and had a soul that communed by mind, will, and emotions. He lived in a body formed and designed by God only for life on earth.

As we observe in our imagination, Father God instructs everyone in heaven's assembly that a healthy spirit requires deep fellowship with Him personally—the Great I Am, the source of spirit life, and the foundation and origin of all life. It is only in communion with the Creator of life that Adam (or any of mankind) could grow and mature spiritually. Adam was made without flaw in the image of God, but he did not have all knowledge and power. He had delegated power. He had much to learn. To accomplish the functions for which he was designed, he needed the fellowship of the spirit. Father and son interacting and sharing daily was of utmost necessity for Adam to grow and mature as a son of the Almighty. He needed the Father's guidance and direction. With Adam's interaction with his Father, he would learn more and more of the Father's character and desire. The character of God, the image of God, and the essence of God is *love*! From the Spirit of God flows joy, peace, patience, gentleness, goodness, faith, and self-control. From the beginning, the Father desired that man be so in tune with Him that he would replicate the image of his Father. Our heavenly Father desired that His children would reflect His glory and act in the character, the faith, and the power of God!

"A healthy body," the Father explains, "requires deep penetration of nutrients from the earth's soil through plants. The body's inner workings on very deep and microscopic levels receives nourishment first via the food consumed from the earth's bounty, an imperative! Also, through the atmosphere, oxygenated air filled with organisms and gases that support life are absolutely essential! Drinking fresh water filled with minerals give support to all the liquids flowing through his body, truly critical! Receiving the sun's healing rays that supply many necessary nutrients for the support of body functions, indispensable! A body that was fearfully and wonderfully made, designed to live in this unique atmosphere, requires so much intricate interaction to be healthy and vibrant." This is a fellowship with the earth and universe in which it was made, a fellowship that is absolutely necessary to life.

Adam possessed these two necessary characteristics in his life. However, in his soul, he was hungry for fellowship with someone on earth like himself, connected to God the Father in the spirit as well. A being resembling himself who could understand, communicate, and interact with him on deeper levels was required. Satisfaction and contentment in his mind, will, and emotions required more than the interactions provided by the animals and plant life in the garden. Like his heavenly Father, Adam also had the desire to replicate himself. All the other life the Father created in the garden multiplied. He too desired to bring forth a family to share his life on earth. Adam was incomplete and unfulfilled in the realm of his soul.

To make Adam complete, God put Adam to sleep. As he slept, the Lord performed the first surgery on man. He took a rib out of Adam and created a woman to walk beside him and share in this life. She was formed from a part of Adam (under his arm) for protection and near his heart to be loved. Her body was uniquely fashioned by the Father to be one with Adam and also a child of God. She was conceived, patterned, and planned so that each would complete the other. Adam awoke. The Father enlightened him about what had happened to Adam while he slept. God brought the woman to Adam. The instant they met, they both knew they were designed for each other as perfect companions to walk in love in this life. It was truly love at first sight! They had a connection in the spirit, both being children of God. They connected in their soul, minds, and hearts, loving and giving to each other. They connected in their bodies, both being formed and fashioned for life on this earth.

Adam said, "This is bone of my bone and flesh of my flesh." All other human lives have flowed from their union.

For quite some time, they enjoyed this wondrous heaven on Earth. Heaven's will done on earth. Heaven's love flowed on earth in a spectacular garden of Eden. Adam and Eve walked together and they both walked with God. Adam declared that they were both delighted in their friendship and life. Love flowed between Adam and Eve. They knew only that which was good. They had absolute trust and confidence in each other. They respected each other. They saw only beauty and good in each other. A covering, an aura of beauty, the glory of God clothed them. They saw no flaws in each other because there were none. Everything their Father made was good! Adam and Eve, at that time, had never experienced any strife or pain. Their hearts, their souls, and their spirits were united in love for God, love for each other, and love for all that God had created.

Together, Adam and Eve directed all the activities within their dominion. They tended the garden with love. What they desired to see, they spoke forth in words following their Father's example. There were no thistles or thorns. Weeds did not exist. Storms or droughts were not known. Rain was not needed in the earth because each day the sun shone and each night the dew watered the land. Rivers flowed around the border of the garden that was their home. Springs and ponds dotted the landscape of magnificent, artistic beauty.

All was peace.
All was perfect.
All was pure.
All was love.

4

Power to Choose

Deception leads to doubt,
And doubt opens a doorway,
A doorway to evil desires,
A doorway to disobedience,
And a doorway to death.

In the stadium of heaven, Adam pauses in his narrative. Each one assembled ponders his words. All are enjoying the family's account that he and the Father had so beautifully recited. What an amazing beginning in heaven's family history! The story of the ages is being told. All are smiling and reveling in the greatness and the goodness of Father God.

As observers in heaven's portals, we are witnessing the recitation of a wondrous and epic account, *Story Time in Heaven*. What a blessing we are privileged to enjoy! Now, back to our story we go.

Adam reaches out a hand to the one seated beside him. She grasps his hand and rises up alongside him. Eve joins Adam, hand in hand, as they continue the story together. They begin to take alternate turns speaking as they share examples of their early days on earth. They recite stories of the fellowship, love, and wonder they enjoyed while living in the garden of Eden. The giant three-dimensional screen opens in heaven each time the story continues. This allows us to enter the scene in amazing ways. We watch history repeat itself, as it were, as each story comes alive in our view. Eve loves telling stories about how they communicated with the animals. The animals were all tame and responded to their direction. Eve spends much time interacting with the variety of creatures roaming their paradise of Eden. Adam is a master gardener who enjoys reciting his experiences in tending the garden. He remarks about how easy planting, growing, and harvesting was in those days. He did not need to till the soil. The ground was so fertile that everything grew with such ease. They enjoyed wonderful, delicious fruits, herbs, nuts, seeds, and all kinds of greens in their diet. They both laughed together often as joy was present constantly. Adam and Eve enjoyed deep love and wonderful fellowship with each other as they shared amazing adventures. They learned unique insights into their Father's perfect designs as they observed the plants, animals, and life all around them. This first earthly couple that ruled in the garden of Eden would only speak their desires, and all plant and animal life responded to their direction. Most of all, both Adam and Eve enjoyed visiting with their heavenly Father in the evenings. They would discuss the joys they experienced and their work in this beautiful garden of love!

Adam informs us that he shared with Eve the instructions and authority that he had been given. Adam told Eve about the Father's one special command not to eat of the fruit from the tree of the knowledge of good and evil. Adam shared this with Eve on more than one occasion. The Father of love repeatedly shared this truth as well during their walks in the cool of the evenings. They were both instructed not to eat of its fruit because it would be poison to their system. The Father said, "In the day you eat of it, you will surely die."

After much time together, sharing and working in beautiful Eden, one ruinous day unfolded as both Adam and Eve were tending the garden together. They were in the center of this amazing flowered oasis. This is the section of the garden where the forbidden tree was planted. Eve was communicating with the animals, as was her habit and desire, while Adam was working out more beautiful designs in the garden. They maintained close proximity to each other as they loved to work side by side. Their hearts flowed as one. Eventually, Eve began talking to one of the beasts in the garden, a serpent. This creature was deceitful, bearing evil intent. Eve conveyed that she did not fully comprehend what was happening. She did not perceive that an evil spirit had invaded this serpent. She was not aware that a trespasser, a foreign invader, entered their kingdom. Eve recounts how she was beguiled and enticed by the serpent's words. Initially, he sowed doubt about the accuracy of what God, the heavenly Father, said. The deceiver inquired, "Can it really be true that God said, 'You shall not eat from any tree of the garden'?" Eve argued, "We can eat of every tree in the garden, except the one in the center. We were not to eat of its fruit. In fact, we were not to even touch it or we would die!" Adam begins elaborating on this account by adding that he realized this was an exaggeration, a distortion of what the Father had said. God did not say that if they "touch it," they will die. Adam confesses to us that though he was there with Eve as she talked to the serpent, he did nothing to correct or to control the situation. The serpent then touched the fruit and nothing happened. It did not die. Seeing this, Eve tentatively reached out her hand. She touched the fruit and nothing happened. She did not die. This action created an unusual feeling Eve had never experienced before! It was scary, fascinating, and exciting! Eve then went on to say that the deceiving serpent said, "Don't you see? You certainly will not die!"

Finally, the serpent led her into the greatest deception of all. He spoke doubt about the character of God. He cast doubt about the Father's intent in commanding them not to eat it. He convinced them that they would be like God, knowing both good and evil, if they ate from this forbidden tree. Eve was confused and deceived by the serpent's words. She was mesmerized by the new feelings she was experiencing. Eve looked away from the Father's love and from the Father's protecting command. Embracing a lie, Eve gave her trust and allegiance to another. She looked at the poisonous fruit. It was beautiful to the eye. It promised new and exciting experiences. The fruit felt wonderful to touch in her hand. Her mouth began to water as she craved for what she never had. Eve desired its wicked promise, a promise that she would be like God. Eve had been seduced by the lying allure of the moment! She then partook of the tree's life-destroying fruit!

Adam, present in that moment with Eve and knowing that God had *not* said touch it and you will die, failed to speak the truth. He failed to exercise his God-given authority over this deceiving invader. Adam had the power to cast the deceiver from the garden with a simple command. He had that authority. Yet he failed to protect that which God had given him authority over in this life! Adam was there with her and knew the serpent was lying. Adam was watching his wife as she was being deceived. Adam was there with the authority, knowledge, and power to obtain the victory. Adam was there, but he failed! His deceived wife passed the forbidden fruit to her husband and he willingly betrayed the entire family! Adam, of his own free will, put his and his wife's will and desire above that of the Creator of life's desire and direction. Adam willingly disobeyed the known will of God!

Instantly, the world changed! Peace fled and turmoil invaded. Health fled as sickness, disease, and death invaded. Joy fled and heartache and sadness invaded. Purity fled and shame and disgrace invaded. Faith fled as fear, doubt, and worry invaded. Adam's authority and dominion fled and an evil, alien spirit invaded and took authority for himself! *He to whom you submit, that is whose servant you are!*

As the giant visual screen in heaven fades, we are again observing heaven's grandstand. All is silent as a hush has overtaken the vast assembly of saints. Seeing this scene, we feel great wonder, sadness, and suspense.

5

Consequence and Covenant

Where sin and disobedience abound,
Grace and mercy will more abound.
What was originally intended for evil,
God will turn for our good.

Heaven's citizens are stunned by the power of this revelation. The actions of that disastrous day have generated a deep heavy silence as all ponder its significance. The gravity of this betrayal cannot be overemphasized! The repercussions vibrate throughout the assembly as the tremors of this terrible tragedy continued on earth ever since that fateful day. Through time and eternity, the destiny of our world has been impacted yet we hear no condemnation for Adam or his failures. Each person in this assembly realizes we were all there with him when it happened. We were all a part of Adam since we all come from him. No matter how many generations later we were born, we have all failed and made similar mistakes.

As an imaginary observer of the scene, I am amazed at the multitudes reaction. Instead of looking in condemnation at Adam and Eve, as many people on earth would often do when observing another's failure, we have a completely unexpected response here in this heavenly grandstand. The entire assembly of citizens, all saints of God and the redeemed of the ages, seem to be looking not at Adam but at the brilliant, golden container before the throne of the Father. This is the incredibly beautiful vessel that seemed so important earlier as we first caught a glimpse of it there before the Father's throne. Each eye appears to be focusing upon the scarlet liquid flowing down its golden sides. Gradually, as they ponder its meaning, all eyes turn their focus, upon the Son of God seated on His throne at the Father's right hand. He is the one with the scars in His hands, His feet, His back, and His side that appear as jewels of healing light. Everyone gazes at Him with such love in their eyes. As we look at the Son of God seated upon His throne, He seems to change shape for just a moment. We try to focus, rub our blurred eyes, and then look more closely. The Son of God momentarily appears as a lamb slain on an altar with blood pouring out. We gasp as we ache in our hearts at this sight! Yet somehow we rejoice in our souls at the same time. In this special moment in this heavenly vision, we realize a provision was made before the problem arose.

As we continue this epic story, Adam and Eve begin to disclose the trouble and transformation in their lives on earth flowing from the consequences of their actions. Adam now reveals that the joy and anticipation they both felt in their daily walk with their Father God changed forever. Their joy turned into fear and their anticipation into anxious dread. *Sin has consequences.* Eve conveys that she no longer had the same fellowship with any of the animals. Her experience with the serpent now tainted her view of all animals. The trust was gone. The love, openness, and trust between Adam and Eve was immediately lost. They had shame and saw their own nakedness and flaws as well as the defects in each other. They lost much of the respect they had for each other. They hid from God and each other. This amazing, loving couple, the world's first love story, turned into a disastrous heartbreak as they began to close their hearts to each other. Both Adam and Eve began to mask their feelings. They tried to cover the stain of sin that was now evident by covering themselves with leaves to hide their self-consciousness and shame. The glory of God that covered them before was lost and left them naked and humiliated. *Sin has consequences.* Adam then reports that the whole earth appears to be in rebellion! He felt things in his body and soul that he never dealt with before. Strange feelings, wrong feelings, and evil feelings. Before the entrance of sin, prior to succumbing to temptation, all he knew was good. Now Adam explains there was a war of good against evil raging within him, a cloud of confusion overshadowed him. Fear and doubt embraced him. A perfect man, who was in perfect fellowship with God and his wife, lost his way completely. Adam forfeited his power, abused his authority, and relinquished his dominion on earth to an alien invader. He could no longer direct the animals. They sensed his fear and fled from him. The plant life that he tended in the garden resisted his normal activity as weeds began to arise and choke out its growth. *Sin has consequences. We do not live in a vacuum with freedom from consequences. The reality of repercussions ripples through the realm of life.* If our family's story was to end here, what a disaster that would be! But the story has only just begun. This black, dark day is not the end.

In the throne room of heaven where the story is being told, Adam and Eve are now quiet as our loving Father begins to enlighten us about the happenings of that day. The visual images before us, reveal that it is now the evening on the first day of man's sin. As the Creator, our heavenly Father's presence appears in the garden, He reminds us this was His daily habit and what He loved to do. He would visit with his son and his daughter each evening. He entered Eden to visit with his family at the appointed time of fellowship already aware of the disaster that had occurred in the garden. He knew the enormity of consequences that Adam and Eve now faced. Neither of them showed up. The two lost souls were hiding from their Father, terrified to see the Creator face-to-face! The Father knew their hiding place among the trees in the garden. He said, "There is no hiding place where you can go that your heavenly Father does not know!" His presence filled all things. His Father asked Adam, "Where are you?" Trembling, Adam answered that he had heard the Father's voice in the garden and was afraid because of his nakedness. That was why he was hiding. The Father inquired how he knew he was naked and asked Adam if he had eaten of the forbidden fruit.

God reveals to us that, like so many since his day, Adam began to blame someone else for his sin. He blamed it on Eve, the woman that had been given to him. "Adam was even trying to partially put blame on me," the Father says. "He inferred it was my fault for even giving the woman to him. When I inquired of Eve what she had done, she tried to transfer the blame as well. Blaming it on the serpent who was so beguiling she could not help but eat the luscious but forbidden fruit." Viewing this in our imagination, we are learning rich, significant truths from the story of our heavenly family. We make a mental note to remember these things when this imaginary journey ends. The Father is sharing some important truths. He explains, "Blaming others is never the answer. Blaming others does not serve as an excuse. Men always live and die by their choices, not the choices of another."

You'll never be your best if you blame your problems on all the rest!
Your choice, not theirs, determines your destiny!

Choices do have consequences, and actions always cause reactions. What is sown, we eventually reap. Sin has consequences. In fact, sin has wages, and the wage paid is death. This truth Adam and Eve are just beginning to see. The Father is explaining this truth to us clearly.

The Father now proclaims that, because of its evil actions, the serpent was cursed above all beasts of the earth. It was forced to go on its belly and eat dust all the days of its life. Opposition and hostility was placed between the woman and the serpent and between their descendants. Then a prophetic statement of hope was made by the Father in the very midst of failure. "The serpent's descendant," He declared, "would bruise the woman's seed, but her seed would crush the serpent's head!" Part of the consequences of Eve's sin would also include the challenges of giving birth and the pains that accompany it. She would still have desire for her husband, but he would rule over her with strength and authority. The battle of the sexes had begun.

From our imaginary viewpoint in heaven's grandstand, we hear the Father informing the assembly of saints of the consequences of Adam's sin of listening to his wife who had been deceived rather than listening to and obeying the Father's clear command. The ground was placed under a curse. What once produced so easily will now grudgingly produce through sorrow and toil all the days of Adam's life. Thorns and thistles will spring up to hinder the production of food. Adam and his family would only eat by the sweat of their brow as they labor each day. This will continue until the day Adam returns to the ground. "From dust I made you," the Father said, "and dust you are and to dust you shall return!"

At this point in the story, the grandstand in heaven is totally silent. The contemplation of Adam's fall—mankind's fall—is so devastating! From dust to God's glorious son was so exciting to hear! But now to hear the words, *back to dust*, how tragic! Though only imaginary observers, all of us on this incredible journey feel like a gigantic balloon of hope has been popped. In an instant, the aura of beauty, life, and hope that filled us with joy and excitement has completely evaporated, disappearing into thin air!

But how amazing is our heavenly Father! We hear the Father declare He was not finished quite yet. He did something significant, something powerful for Adam and Eve just before He banished them from the garden of Eden. The Father of love gave them hope and a way back! The Father took the life of a pure, innocent animal, shed the blood of this lamb, and poured it on the ground from which Adam came. The wages of sin is death. Adam would eventually die physically when his spirit and soul are separated from his body. He had already died spiritually when his spirit was separated from its close fellowship with the Father. On this first day of man's sin, the Father of love instituted a blood covenant with Adam. The blood of the slain lamb would cover their sin. The skin of this slain animal was used as a covering for Adam and Eve to cover their nakedness. This blood covenant included a promise that one day another perfect man would be born who would not fail. This second, Adam would be a descendant of Eve, not Adam. He would give His life as a sacrifice to pay for Adam's sin and indeed for all of Adam's family who would believe in Him! God already determined, long before time began, prior to Adam's sin and failure ever occurred, that He would save Adam on credit. That is, that Adam and his descendants would be given a second chance. This would only happen *if* they would bring the required offering to God at the appointed times, the covenant offering that symbolized the death of this second Adam. By the blood of this innocent animal, their sin would be covered for a year. This animal's blood did not have the power to cleanse them from sin, but the Father would apply it to their account to cover their sin until this second Adam accomplished His sacrifice. "This second Adam," the Father of love declares, "is at my right hand even now! He is my eternal Son! Conferring before the beginning of time, He was willing to become a second Adam and give His life to pay for man's sin. He is the Lamb, slain—as it were—from the foundation of the world. Before Adam was ever born, this provision was already made in the mind and heart of Almighty God!"

Suddenly, the hallelujahs of Praise erupt in heaven. Adam is praising the Lamb of God! Eve is praising the Lamb of God! Saints of all ages are praising the Lamb of God. He provides the second chance, the opportunity for a fresh start for this entire heavenly family. Failure has been turned into victory! The rejoicing is glorious, almost deafening in its volume of thanksgiving and praise. Observing this scene, my eyes fill with tears of joy! My heart sings with the saints of all ages! This same Lamb of God died for you and me!

6

Divine Intervention

A continuing downward spiral
Is incredibly difficult to break.
The speed is increasing faster and faster
With succeeding choices that men make.
Often divine intervention
Provides the only effective brakes!

Story Time in Heaven continues as Adam and Eve rise to their feet again. The visual screen appears, allowing us to view into their world as they are enlightening us about what followed. Yes, immediately following the first day of man's sin. Before they had known and perceived only good, but now they were confronted daily with evil. Toiling each day, we now observe, was so much different for Adam. He who had once known only peace, power, and perfection now knew great difficulty. The ground grudgingly gave forth its fruit with toil as we survey the sweat pouring from his brow. There now was discord and a lack of harmony between him and Eve. The expressions of love so evident before have turned to strife and often disdain. They had been banned from the garden of Eden. Sadly, they could no longer be trusted to heed the Father's instructions and to obey. An angel with a flaming sword guarded and protected the way to the tree of life. The Father of love did not want Adam to eat of the tree of life and continually live in this fallen, degraded state. Something far better had been provided.

Eve tells us how much this first couple initially loved each other, though now their relationship often appeared strained. The unity of the spirit was gone. Connection and loving fellowship was more difficult to embrace. They did find pleasure in their family. God commanded them to be fruitful and fill the earth with their descendants. Year after year, they had children together and told them of the garden of Eden and the origin of their lives. They instructed them clearly of the proper way to contact and commune with God. They were clearly told how to prepare the required covenant offering for sin. Some of their children heeded this instruction; unfortunately, many did not. The war that raged between good and evil in their father and mother now raged within each of them as well.

As Adam and Eve are seated, our Father in heaven continues the narrative. Appearing before us on the screen is a new story. The heavenly Father describes the interaction between two of Adam's sons. These two were making an offering to God on the prescribed day of sacrifice. Abel made the sacrifice of an animal as required by God. The lamb's blood was shed and poured out upon the ground. The animal itself was burned upon an altar. The Father gave His blessing on the sacrifice given. Cain, his brother, brought the fruit of his own labor to the altar. He offered it in place of the blood covenant sacrifice. No blood was shed, no forgiveness was given. The Father clearly instructed that without the shedding of blood, there is no forgiveness of sin. The Father did not give His blessing to Cain. This made Cain angry toward God and his brother. Hatred arose in his heart. We see the heavenly Father talking with Cain about his offering. God said, "You know what sacrifice is acceptable to Me. Do not be so angry. If you offer the acceptable sacrifice, you will be accepted. If you don't, if you ignore my instructions, sin is crouching at your door. It desires to overpower you but you must master it!" Unfortunately, Cain did not heed the word of the heavenly Father. He nursed his hurt, magnified and criticized the rejection of the offering, and became bitter toward God and his brother Abel. One day, his heart exploded in rage. He became the first murderer as he took his brother's life! The heavenly Father shares that the spiral of sin continued. One after another, men seemed to go in their own way. The beauty of His masterpiece, the purpose of His entire creative miracle was being degraded. Rather than reflecting the Father of love, they now began to bear the reflection of the planet's alien invader. The glory of God that was to be shown in the character and life of man was now degraded, made unholy and repulsive to the God of love. The image of God was almost totally lost to man. The earth was becoming laden with sin. Fear came over all of creation. After about fifteen hundred Earth years, the billions that now lived on the planet had become absolutely depraved. They were a stench in the nostrils of God. Man was debased and degenerate, no longer filled with love, joy, and purity, but now filled with lust, hate and evil desires. Men lost their direction, their purpose, and their way completely.

On heaven's viewing screen, we see lewd, wicked, coarse, and vulgar men and women. We hear filthy language, lewd and evil practices, and hate-filled actions from everyone. Seeing all of this, the Father now regretted that He had ever made man. He was grieved in His heart. The heavenly Father declares to everyone gathered in the grandstand that He planned to destroy everything that He made. Man's sin and debauchery, this disgusting, evil state was totally unacceptable to the Holy God. As the Father shares this, you could have heard a pin drop in heaven. The assembled multitudes around the throne are quiet. The silence is deafening.

At the Father's direction, another family member stands to address the heavenly throng. He begins to recount how he lived at that time and how he was concerned by all that was happening. The evil and wickedness of his day grieved him greatly. He sought the Father, sacrificed in the manner that had been passed on to him from his father. He followed the blood covenant instructions. In that dark and evil day, he said, "I found grace and favor in the eyes of the Lord. I walked in fellowship with the Father like my great-grandfather Enoch had done." He introduced himself to the assembly as Noah and mentioned that he had three sons born to him in that difficult time. "One day," Noah expresses, "God the Father shared his plan to destroy these evil men and to make a fresh start. He instructed me to make a gigantic wooden boat or an ark, coat it inside and out with a waterproof substance, and construct many pens, cages, stalls, and compartments inside it. He gave me the blueprint and the exact dimensions. It was made three decks high. The interior was to have a place for all the pairs of animals, birds, and reptiles that the Father would direct to come to him on the day we were to enter the ark. Instructions were given to take provisions and fill the storerooms on the ark once it was finished. These provisions would be used to feed our family and the many varieties of animal pairs that the Father directed to the ark. This project was a major task that took many, many years—in fact, many decades—to complete. No one had ever constructed anything like this before! Noah said, "I suppose you can imagine what people thought of what I was doing. None of them believed that a flood would come because it had never even rained. God was going to flood the entire world and destroy every man and beast upon it."

Only Noah himself fellowshipped with God in the covenant of love. None of his generation sacrificed in the prescribed manner that the Father instituted on the first day of man's sin. None but Noah could then truly hear the voice of God. Noah acquaints us with the ridicule he endured as we see them mocking him, scoffing him, and cursing him. They laughed him to scorn and discounted the entire fool-hardy project. "To them," Noah informs us, "I was a fool, a buffoon, and an ignorant religious radical. But the God of heaven considered me a preacher of righteousness. Because I believed His word, I was deemed righteous. It was all by faith." Looking around at the vast millions in this stadium and in the presence of angels, archangels, and the twenty-four elders on their thrones, Noah said, "It is a devastating thing to have to reveal this fact. My family and I are the only ones from my generation present here before the throne of the Almighty God."

Wow, unbelievable! Such a tragic statement we have just heard! Noah's generation had not only lost out on the blessing of God in their time, but for all eternity! *Choices have eternal consequences.*

Noah continues, "When the day came, God instructed me to go into the ark. Though others had seen the work I was doing, none of them changed their wicked ways or called upon God. Of all the people on the earth, only I was obedient and righteous in my entire generation. I was instructed to go inside the ark with my wife, my three sons, and their wives. I was to house the animals in the allocated stalls and compartments. Seven pairs of every clean animal and one pair of every unclean animal boarded the ark. Of birds, I was to house seven pair of each in cages. The provisions for food were all loaded and stored. We entered the ark seven days before the flood began. Once everyone was settled in their place, God the Father Himself closed the door behind us. He sealed us in to protect us from the danger outside."

The flood was a terrifying experience! What happened in the next days was calamitous. As the rain began, the earth opened as well. The fountains of the deep began to burst. They bubbled and cast up water onto the earth with great force. Cataclysmic earthquakes shifted the earth's surface. Huge fissures opened as massive separations of land surfaces created deep ravines. The land itself moved in spasms, changing its configuration. Tectonic plates moved, the land mass broke apart, and hot lava rose from the depths of the earth. As the ground convulsed, it went through many stages of dramatic transformation. It was as though the very earth itself was repulsed by man's sin. It was convulsing, shaking, and purging itself from the weight of wickedness that it had borne for so long. Mountains erupted as heat and fire rose from the center of the earth and burst forth in streaming molten lava. The crust of the earth trembled; as huge, hot geysers of water spewed into the atmosphere. Above, the heavens opened. Heavy rain poured, thunder roared, and lightning flashed. These awe-inspiring atmospheric and terrifying seismic activities had never been seen before. In the first few hours, we heard the cries and curses of the wicked outside the ark. Sadly, their day of salvation had passed and the day of judgment had arrived. Continuing forty days, this horrific storm covered the entire earth. The planet itself seemed in turmoil. Tornados, hurricane force winds, rain from above, and hot geysers spouting water from beneath mingled together, filling the entire earth. The surface of the earth was completely engulfed in water. First the lowlands and valleys, then the plains and the high plains, and then one mountain range after another until the entire world was covered with water. The water rose so high that it was many feet above the very highest mountains. All life on the earth was destroyed. Not a soul outside the ark, whether man or beast, survived this onslaught of terror. The visualization of this catastrophic and epic flood is amazing to see on the screen in the grandstand of heaven. We are in awe!

Noah relates, "As the waters rose, so did our ark. The plan of God is always perfect. The Lord was our refuge, our hiding place from all the turmoil around us. His instructions for building the ark were perfect. It was designed for our good. As we followed His plan, we were saved. When the Father shut the door, He sealed us inside, providing complete safety. In the ark, we floated above all the upheaval and turmoil outside. After forty days of raining steadily, combined with the underground waters coming up, the Father made the wind blow over the earth. The doors to the underground waters and the windows of heaven were closed as the rain ceased. For five months, the water slowly receded. As it receded, the floodwaters eroded rocks, sculpted landscapes, molded valleys, and gradually filled the deep fissures of the newly separated lands, creating huge lakes and oceans. Eventually, the landscape settled in the configuration the Father designed for His renewed earth. The Father himself would now set the boundaries for the oceans once they receded completely. The wind blew steadily, drying and shaping the earth as well. After those five months, much of the water had drawn back to its place. Our ark came to rest on the mountains of Ararat. Three more months as the waters continued to recede, we remained safe in the ark. By this time, we could look out from the ark and see the tops of surrounding mountains. We waited another forty days then we sent out a raven. Later we sent out a dove but it found no place to rest and returned to the ark. Seven days later, we sent the dove out again. This time, it returned carrying an olive leaf. We now knew the earth was drying and beginning to produce again. Seven days later, we released the dove one more time and were pleased when it did not return. We waited patiently for many months as the earth dried. Finally, the day arrived when the earth had returned to fruitfulness and plant life was beginning to bloom and grow. We had been protected, and God had provided for all our needs! We had been upon the ark for more than an entire year. God said to me, 'Go out of the ark!'

"We opened the door, stepping out onto dry ground. The earth was purged and purified from its evil stench! As my family walked out together, creatures great and small following behind, it was an awesome experience. We entered into a bright new world! Nothing appeared as we remember before the flood. Everything felt fresh, clean, and alive. We thanked our Father God for His provision, protection, faithfulness, and grace. Our first act upon leaving the ark was to build an altar where we offered a blood covenant sacrifice of Thanksgiving to our heavenly Father. We took one of every clean animal and bird. They were killed. Their blood was shed and poured upon the newly purged earth. Their bodies were burned on the altar as an offering to God. This was the instructions of the Father to Adam, and to His descendants, following Adam's sin, in the garden. The wages of sin, the penalty for sin, is death. From the beginning, this truth has been known. The life of all flesh is in the blood of that animal. Without the shedding of blood, which brings death, no sin can ever be erased. It was our only access to fellowship with God."

Although we did not know it at that time, Noah's informs us on that altar he and his family were looking forward to another sacrifice, the sacrifice of a Lamb slain from the foundation of the world. It was by His grace; that Noah and his family were saved. It was done on credit, looking forward to a sacrifice that would one day would be made. What a beautiful image of Noah and his family in the newly created world, worshipping around the altar. Somehow we can feel in our hearts from our place as observers that the Father has been pleased with Noah's story. We can sense the Father gazing at the beautiful golden box in front of His throne and the scarlet liquid flowing down its sides.

As the image of the renewed earth emerges before us, Noah informs us that the Father made a promise that He would never flood the earth the same way again. He gave an awesome sign of His promise as a brilliant rainbow spread across the sky overhead. God's promise of new beginnings was magnificent! Observing Noah in our imaginary journey, we see a rainbow of even greater depth and color surrounding the heavenly Father's throne. The promise on earth was but a reflection of the promise recorded in eternity. There is always a promise of grace and hope when facing trouble or turmoil for those who hear and follow the voice of God in faith. The promise, unfortunately, is not for all; it's *only* for all who will believe. Millions perished in the terror of the flood because they ignored and disobeyed the call of God. There was a way established by the Creator for our good and His glory, but it must be His way, not ours. Only Noah and his family lived to see the beauty of the rainbow and the recreated earth.

Noah declares, "The Father blessed both me and my family. He told us to be fruitful and multiply on the earth."

The Father promised this as well. "While the earth remains, Seedtime and harvest, Cold and heat, Winter and summer, And day and night Shall not cease" (Gen. 8:22, KJV).

7

First Intermission

Pausing for reflection,
Pausing for praise,
Pausing for introspection,
Prepares us for better days.

Story Time in Heaven has paused. No one is addressing the assembled throng. Some are leaving, some are visiting others, and some are returning with new arrivals to the city. This is just an intermission, a time to catch our breath and reflect. I am truly thankful for the break. There is so much to digest.

My family often said, "When I get to heaven, I'm going to ask." Then they would name a Bible character, desiring to know in more detail certain things about their lives. Perhaps that is what some are doing in the heavenly throne room right now. Saints from all ages are present, conversing about the stories we have witnessed and perhaps sharing with each other some of the wonderful events of their lives on earth. In this moment, my personal desire is to reflect on all we have seen and heard here in heaven. The spirit is our guide on this heavenly journey. He fills in the blanks where we lack understanding. I realize, being in a place that is forever day, we may not understand many things.

Story Time in Heaven has been on center stage. We are informed in the spirit, however, that the heavenly Father is not just aware of what we are witnessing as we hear and see these epic adventures. As the story progresses, our Father is still focused on every earthly soul at the very same time. What an incredible revelation! On earth, we think of someone who can multitask as an individual who could accomplish multiple things at a time. God the Father; His precious Son, Our Lord; and the Holy Spirit of God are the ultimate multitasker! He is present in every situation for every individual at any given moment on earth, just as He is present here in eternity. The volume of His knowledge is inexhaustible. His power has no limit. His love knows no bounds. His presence is in every location, whether it be in time or eternity. His presence fills all things. Nothing exists outside of His knowledge, power, love, and presence. What an awe-inspiring revelation that in the midst of all that is happening on earth and in eternity, we can each clearly know and say with assurance that God is thinking about me!

During this intermission in our imagination, we are taken outside the stadium. We are guided up and down golden avenues and are reminded of our initial entrance to this glorious city. When we first arrived in heaven everything seemed such a blur! Multitudes of images bombarded our senses. We are only now reminded of how amazing the approach to heaven had been. We initially embarked on this imaginary journey from planet earth, as in the spirit we left our earthly bodies and traveled to areas outside of time and beyond the realm of space and entered this glorious place called heaven. What we failed to describe and must acknowledge is the magnificent appearance of heaven as we approached it on this grand expedition. Drawing near to the magnificent celestial city called heaven from across the blackness and far reaches of eternity, its appearance is of glowing, golden light, more brilliant and pure than the sun. This is not a blinding but rather an illuminating brightness. There is an indescribable richness, clarity, and beauty that boggles the mind as we endeavor to express what we behold. The luminous, warm glow is unlike any other light. Radiant, pure and transparent in its effect.

The light of the city we know is the glory and presence of God Himself. As this eternal light streams from His throne, it passes through the entire city. This glorious living, and loving, light flows through the streets and mansions touching every part of the celestial city. Heaven is brilliantly lit; colorful, yet transparent at the same time! In our approach to heaven we noticed massive walls around the city that appear to be about fifteen hundred miles long and fifteen hundred miles wide! These walls are constructed of precious gems varying in color and hue and perfectly cut to reflect and refract the multitude of colors displayed all around. Emerald green, amber, sapphire blue, ruby reds, and so many more colors that are clear and transparent allowing the light of the eternal heavenly Father to flow through them as they honor His beauty and glory! We observe twelve main foundational jewels. Each one reflects its own dynamic and diverse shades of color. On each side of the four walls surrounding this vast city we see three massive gates. Each gate is made of one large pearl of great beauty and value. The gate is translucent in appearance and always remains open. It is never night in this city. Drawing near to the gate we see a powerful, winged, warrior angel guarding the gate holding a flaming sword in his hand. Every gate is guarded by one of the magnificent angels. These guardians of heaven's entrance have access to a record containing the names of heaven's citizens. Only citizens are authorized to enter this magnificent place. The database containing these names is referred to as the Lamb's Book of Life.

Above each gate allowing access to heaven portals, a name is inscribed. Each of the exquisite, foundational gem stones is named as well. There are twenty-four names, twelve above the gates and twelve engraved on the foundation stones. Somehow, we perceive that the individuals whose names are engraved, will be a part of the narrative told during *Story Time in Heaven*. The celestial city itself is not just one level. It is approximately fifteen hundred miles high so that the length, width, and height are equal and from a distance, this heavenly city looks like a glorious, glowing cube of light, life, and color! Back within the city, we notice as we pass by that each magnificent mansion lining the streets is unique. Not a single duplicate is found. How impressive and fascinating to see the structural variations! Even more fascinating is that their diversity does not clash, but complements and enhances the beauty of the other structures around them. We are told that each person is an absolute original. Each one has traveled their own peculiar pathway before arriving in heaven. The Father knows each one intimately. Their individual mansion has been prepared for them by His personal design. If a snowflake, a fingerprint, a voice print, and DNA is unique to individuals on earth, how much more all things prepared for us in heaven are uniquely individual as well. The city of heaven is so vast where streets are layered hundreds of levels high! Long grand avenues as far as the eye can see stretch in every direction, yet within the vast space enclosed by its outer walls this city is expanding and enlarging constantly. Life is short on earth. When earth's test is done, a place in heaven is prepared for those who believe. People leave earth each day by the thousands. Sadly, not all arrive in heaven. It doesn't take time, it's an instant transfer! The Father always knows well ahead of time and all things are prepared for their arrival.

Upon their departure from earth, heaven's newest entrants are escorted to the celestial city by their guardian angels who watched over and protected them during their journey on earth. They are led to a beautiful park where those who knew them on earth greet them first. The joy expressed is glorious. Embraces of love greet every victorious saint of God who arrives. Reminiscing, rejoicing, and laughing are some of the amazing interactions we observe. These new citizens were transferred to heaven in the spirit, but they are not in glorified bodies quite yet. However, we are informed that a special day is coming when their bodies and spirits will be reunited! It is a day ahead when mortals put on immortality. These new entrants to the city are led to the individual mansions their heavenly Father has prepared. Everyone has a story, reflecting the glory of God. Sometimes it is their accounts that are recited during *Story Time in Heaven*.

As we consider all we have heard and seen thus far, our hearts are filled with praise for our Creator. We praise Him for the beauty and grandeur of heaven. We praise Him for the beauty of the universe He made. What magnificent detail of design. The interconnectivity of all things always point us to the Father, and we give Him all the glory and praise! The more we see, the more we learn! Seeing the incredibly inspiring detailed design, we are deeply in awe of the magnificence of our Father and praise Him!

At this moment, we are vividly aware that though we can imagine this incredible vision. We are not fully there! The ones whose stories are told have already finished their course on the earth. However, our unique journey cannot be told in heaven's grandstand. Our personal story is not yet finished. We are here in the spirit of our imagination to catch a vision of heavenly things. Our personal mansion is not fully ready. Our journey on earth will eventually continue until the story is complete. Then we will be welcomed to our heavenly home joining the assembly in heaven's throne room. It is then our story may also be told.

When the vision is over, when the imaginary journey is done, may we more intelligently walk upon earth in the brilliant light of eternity.

8

Foundations of Faith

Some people say, "Faith is a leap,"
That "it's going way out on a limb."
But the truth is, it's simply a step
Of putting our trust in Him.

We are told intermission is over. We must continue *Story Time in Heaven*. Moving toward the throne room, we follow the crowd. Many among them were new arrivals. The new entrants of heaven are excited as we are to hear the greatest stories ever told, the story of the ages recounted by those who lived them, the stories of our heavenly family, and, most of all, the story of God's grace! As we move into our place as observers, we see the city growing larger and the stadium of heaven along with it! All are entering the Father's presence with thanksgiving. They are entering his courts with praise. There is singing, shouting, dancing, and rejoicing! Everyone is incredibly excited as they approach the throne of God's grace. The songs of angels, heaven's choir, mingle with instruments of every kind. Stringed instruments—woodwinds, trumpets, and trombones—are accompanied with percussion, cymbals, and drums. Together, they magnify the Father and the glorious Son. As the angels sing, the saints of all ages blend in, taking us to places of the heart where music has never penetrated before. Our hearts, our souls, and our spirits explode in exuberant praise! The magnificent chorus went on forever it seemed, yet no one wanted it to end. On earth, none have ever experienced a musical event that could compare.

Our heavenly Father is pleased with the offering of praise. We feel His love burning deeply within our hearts. The Father then hushes the crowd. Every eye in heaven turns to the throne of grace. He directs the next speaker to stand. One of the twenty-four elders seated on a throne facing the throne of God stands up. Now his story will be shared with the congregation of the redeemed. This speaker really needs no introduction. On earth, he has been called for centuries *the friend of God*. As Abraham addresses the assembly, all are on the edge of their seats. He is not only the friend of God, he is considered a father of the faith as well. Abraham recounted that his birth name was Abram and that he was a descendent of Noah, born about three hundred years after the massive flood and after the fresh start was given to mankind. A few more instructions were given to man as he exited the ark to start a new life. Until this time, both man and beast were vegetarians. Now the heavenly Father allowed men to consume some of the animals as well. One of the instructions they received after leaving the ark of safety was to be fruitful and repopulate the earth. This he was told by his ancestors but, unfortunately, they did not fully obey. As they grew greatly in number, men wanted to stay together to build great cities reaching to heaven and to make a name for themselves, rather than to obey God.

In those first generations after the flood, many men had already forgotten or perverted the blood covenant sacrifice. They left the way of truth and embraced their desires and the desires of the alien invader rather than the direction of their Creator. As they planned to build cities to the skies for their own glory; God knew what He placed within them. He knew the power, that unity of purpose and power of agreement possessed. He understood that their selfish, rebellious purpose would lead to unrestrained evil and rebellion on earth. One day, everyone on earth woke up confused. They could not communicate with each other. The heavenly Father confused the language of the earth's entire population. He then scattered them across the face of the earth.

"My ancestors settled in a city named Ur of the Chaldeans," Abram said. "That is where I was born. Though many in my day did not worship God, my heart wanted to know and to follow Him." Abram continues the story of how his father had taken them to another city called Haran, intending to go all the way to Canaan. In Haran, his father died. Shortly afterward, he says, "God spoke to me. He told me to leave my country and my relatives and go to a land that He would show me. If I followed Him, the Father would make of me a great nation and bless me abundantly. He would make my name great, and I would be a blessing to many others. God said He would bless everyone who blessed me, and curse anyone who cursed me. In me, all the families of the earth would be blessed. What an incredible promise! I believed in my heart what God said. With my wife Sarai and my nephew Lot, I took my first steps of faith. When we arrived in the land the Father sent us, it was so beautiful. I felt His blessing and approval. Over the years, we moved to a variety of places within the land and each place we stopped, I built an altar. There we sacrificed an offering to the Lord, our heavenly Father. This method, which God established for man to worship Him, was passed down all the way from Adam. God said, 'Without the shedding of blood, there was no forgiveness for sin." At first, I had little understanding of why. I believed and obeyed what He said. Eventually, I gained much greater revelation in visions and in my fellowship with the Lord."

"During my journey," Abram recounts, "God blessed me in so many ways. No matter where I wandered, my wealth in all things increased. It was just as He had promised in Haran. I, as other men, was not perfect in all things. I made mistakes, sometimes through fear or lack of patience. But God was always there, and I always repented and worshiped God's way. What I have found so amazing about my friend, our heavenly Father, is that even though I made mistakes, when my heart was right, He still turned them around for my good! As I journeyed with the Lord, He shared with me many more promises! One time, He had me look over the entire land from a high point (to the north, south, east, and west). He told me that this entire area would be my descendant's land. Then he shared that my descendants would be as numerous as the dust of the earth. I was awed by the magnitude of that promise. My nephew Lot settled in fertile plains near a city named Sodom. One day, Sodom and other cities around were attacked by the kings of five different cities and lost. One of the consequences of the battle was that Lot and his possessions were captured. When word arrived to me of their capture, I armed the three hundred eighteen men of my household and together we pursued their captors. Though we were greatly outnumbered by the five kings, we attacked and defeated them in the strength of the Lord! The Lord fought the battle with us and He destroyed our enemies! We brought back Lot, his people, and all their possessions." Abram smiles as he fills us in about one very special moment in his life following the victory that day. "The king of Salem (ancient Jerusalem) brought bread and the fruit of the vine to nourish us. He was a priest of the Most High God, our heavenly Father. Melchizedek was his name. He blessed me in the name of God Most High, Creator and Possessor of heaven and earth, and he acknowledged that it was God who delivered my enemies into my hand!"

As Abram recounts his story about Melchizedek, I noticed he was looking directly at Jesus, the Son of God who was seated on His throne. There was a smile on the face of Jesus as He gazed back at Abraham. This gave me pause.

Not long after this, Abram continues, "God spoke to me in a vision. He declared Himself to be my shield and my protector. The Lord God proclaimed that my reward would be very great. My response in the vision was to ask the Lord God what reward I could have when I didn't even have any children. I reminded the Lord that my servant would be my heir because I had no son. Then the Lord told me to go outside of my tent that night and look at the stars. He said, 'If you can count the stars, you can count the number of your descendants!' As I stepped outside the tent, I walked a few hundred yards away to a place where there was no competing earthly light. There the heavens were displayed in all their beauty above me. Constellations, galaxies, and stars—millions of stars! What beauty and grandeur! On this crystal clear, cloudless night, God's glory mesmerized me! As I saw the power of what God's words alone created and reflected on the promise the Lord had just made to me, how could I ever doubt Him? I believed what God said. Faith bloomed in my heart. God also considered me righteous because I believed. He reminded me that he brought me from Haran and had been with me and blessed me in all that I did. He said I would have a son of my own. The Lord God and I then renewed and strengthened the blood covenant first introduced in the garden of Eden."

As we listen to the story, knowledge is imparted to us in the spirit. We begin to understand new truths and gain greater understanding about what constitutes a blood covenant. We perceive that a blood covenant seals two people or groups of people (like families or tribes) to a powerful commitment. Each one pledges all they possess and all they are, is at the disposal of their covenant partner. A covenant partner is the deepest of friendships, closer than even the kinship of a brother by birth. Abram was always regarded as the friend of God. All that Abram possessed belonged to God. In return, God promised the same to Abram. If either had a need of any type, they could freely call upon each other on the basis of the blood covenant. It is a very solemn agreement. To ratify the covenant, Abram was instructed to take three animals. They were to be split in half and their blood was shed. It was then poured into the ground from which man was made. The word *blood covenant* means "to cut where blood flows." Each party to the covenant walked between the two halves and encircled them in a figure eight. The two halves of each animal represented that the two partners were now becoming one. The figure eight was a symbol of eternity, the never-ending length of their pledge. A great darkness fell over the place that night where the covenant sacrifice was laid. As Abram encircled the animals, the Lord showed Abram a burning lamp like a smoking furnace as the fire of God Almighty passed between the pieces as well. God himself was meeting Abram and confirming the covenant. Abram revealed that while they were making this covenant, they made pledges to each other. The Lord God also shared prophetic words and visions concerning the future of Abram's family. God said Abram's family would eventually travel out of this land into Egypt. While there, they would be enslaved and oppressed for four hundred years. God promised that He would eventually bring judgment on that nation and that they would come out of this time of slavery with great possessions. The Lord pledged that after they came out of Egypt, Abram's descendants would inherit this land, where he now resided. The area would belong to Abram's seed forever, from the river of Egypt to the great river Euphrates!

"When I was ninety-nine years old, the Lord appeared to me again. He renewed the covenant and made it even stronger. He changed my name from Abram to Abraham, which means, 'father of many nations.' In my old age and my wife Sarai past childbearing age, He promised us a son together. Sarai's name was changed to Sarah or princess. She would be a mother of nations, and kings of people would come from her. The Lord also became known as the God of Abraham! Exchanging of names is another covenant principle. Each covenant partner had the authority of each other's family name. The Lord and I made many promises to each other that day. We deepened and strengthened our covenant of blood as we instituted circumcision upon every male in our family. This was another sign and seal of our covenant together. At the appointed time, our son Isaac was born. His name means 'laughter.' He brought great joy to us from his birth. God did a miracle for Sarah and me," Abraham said. "What was beyond the power or ability of our bodies because of our age, God accomplished through the promise of His Word. When we believe his Word, the words themselves have creative power. All the universe was created and is sustained…by His Word!" To all the assembled family in heaven's grandstand, Abraham declares that all through his life, every promise He made, the Lord kept! "He is faithful. He is trustworthy. He alone is worthy of praise!"

At this point, hallelujahs break out in heaven's throne room. Everyone is glorifying God! Abraham, the friend of God, declared that faith in God is *not* a leap into the unknown, it is simply standing on the rock of God's Word. By His Word, He created all things. By His Word, He sustains all things. When you trust in His Word, there is no surer footing in heaven, on earth, or in the entire universe. *Amens* ring out in heaven. Saints of all ages praise God. A thunderous roar is heard as an explosion of thanksgiving and praise bursts forth.

Everyone is crying out, "Glory and honor and praise be unto our God!"

As observers of this vision, we begin to realize that everyone who is now praising God with such energy and enthusiasm, had experienced the same faithfulness of God themselves while they walked their earthly journey. This is a congregation of victors and overcomers, and they overcame by the blood of the Lamb and the word of their testimony. *All who came* to heaven came by the same pathway of faith.

9

Faith Tested

Three days journey with a heavy heart.
Three days journey in a test of faith.
Three days journey that revealed God's heart.
Three days journey sealed the believer's fate.

There are so many stories yet to be told in heaven's grandstand, however, Abraham has one more account in his experience to share before he yields the speaker's podium to others. Personally, I imagine that it would be amazing just to hear more of Abraham's incredible stories of faith.

Abraham recounts the delight he experienced when his son Isaac was born. At the time of his birth, Abraham was a hundred years old! Sarah was very old as well. This promised baby was a miracle from the Lord God. Isaac was circumcised on the eighth day of his life as a symbol of the covenant relationship between God and Abraham, which extended to succeeding generations in Abraham's family. As Isaac grew, his father Abraham loved him more each day. He shared with Isaac his relationship with the Lord God. He taught his son about the sins of their ancestors, beginning with Adam. He taught him about the repercussions and consequences of that sin and how death had entered the human family. Isaac became familiar with the requirement of a covenant sacrifice at the prescribed times. The covenant was shared and expanded upon from Adam right up to their time. Abraham was very clear in his teaching of Isaac. His son knew their only hope of prosperity and blessing in this life leading to eternal life was through faith and obedience to the blood covenant.

Isaac is now standing beside his father Abraham in the throne room of heaven. He is assisting in telling the next part of their story. They both disclose various aspects of their life as Isaac grew into a young man. Love and fellowship between father and son grew daily. Abraham loved his son. Everyone could see the closeness and love between them. Abraham knew—and God had assured him—that through Isaac, this miracle child of promise, the Lord would bless and reward him. Abraham's family would grow, prosper, and eventually bring great blessing to all nations of the world. Abraham and Isaac worked alongside each other. Isaac was being groomed to eventually take over the family assets and continue the family business. His father was very wealthy. They had a large staff and many assets. All that they had was fully surrendered to God. It was the Lord who blessed them mightily. They recognized His ownership of all their assets by giving a tithe. They gave 10 percent back to the Lord.

Standing in the assembly of the saints of God from all ages and before the throne of the God of heaven and earth, Abraham pauses. He looks first toward his dear Lord and Friend seated upon the throne. He then casts his gaze toward the Son of God seated at the Father's right hand. Abraham pauses, smiles, and then gives attention to the golden covenant vessel before God's throne. Abraham surveys the scarlet liquid flowing down the sides of this sacred vessel. As we observe Abraham's actions, an image appears of three crosses upon a hill with the Son of God nailed to the center cross.

Until this point in our account of *Story Time in Heaven*, I have not attempted to share the complete fullness of the vision we are seeing in our imagination. As the stories unfold before us, so much more is taking place than can be fully recounted. Not knowing quite how to describe the scene, let me just say this. During these accounts, images appear before the throne in the center of this vast stadium of heaven on what I can only describe as a three-dimensional screen. Yet there is nothing to block the view from any direction. This is a three-hundred-sixty-degree, three-dimensional image. No actual screen exists. It is as though we have stepped into the story. Everyone in the stadium can see the images clearly. The images just miraculously appear as the speakers are sharing their accounts. The display, for our benefit, is a magnificent panorama of light, color, smell, and sound! Everything that our ears hear, our eyes see. It would be like a hologram on earth, only far more advanced. *Story Time in Heaven* is enhanced beyond the best visual effects of any movie on earth. This is not just the story line conveyed in words. This is not the whimsical, deceptive, and imaginative work of man's storytelling on screen. We effectively see each story in real time. We feel the emotions and hear the speaker's words and the sounds all around the scenes being portrayed. Each of us can smell the aroma of the scenes too! As the adventures are recounted, it is as though we are transported directly and completely into the heart of the scene itself.

Heaven is incredible! It is perpetually day. There is no past; there is no future. Life in heaven is outside of time and space. God the Father knew the end of each story before the story ever began!! Here in heaven, we seem to be tapping right into the stories told at the very moment they were happening on earth. This is astounding! We understand that every word ever spoken, every act ever committed has been—and continues to be—recorded in heaven. There is nothing hidden that cannot be revealed. Long before the Internet or cloud technology on earth, our Father stored everything in the data banks of heaven. Nothing can be done by man to delete or remove them from heaven's memory. We have not only heard with our ears, we are literally seeing everything each speaker talks about. Then our eyes fall upon the golden covenant container covered with the scarlet liquid. We realize there is only one thing powerful enough to erase negative records in heaven's data banks.

The image of the three crosses now disappears from our view. As Abraham continues his narration, we see a scene developing on earth. God appears to Abraham at his home near the end of the day. Abraham's home is a large tent among a small city of tents. The Lord calls out Abraham's name. "Here I am," Abraham responds. God instructs his friend, his covenant partner, to take his only son Isaac, the son that Abraham loved so much. He is told to take him to the land of Moriah. There he is to offer his son Isaac as a burnt offering upon an altar. This altar is to be on a mountain that God specifically chose. The Lord will lead him directly to the correct place. This journey will take about three days.

From an earthly view, this would seem to be an absolutely absurd request. If the bounds of our perspective included only earthly realities, our mind would definitely go tilt. We would scream out that the request from God was unacceptable! Of course, many who do not walk by faith or live in the light of eternity declare *any* demand by God is unacceptable. Abraham was not that type of individual. He knew the Lord as his Friend. He understood the covenant and the absolute certainty of the promises of God. The Lord God Himself promised that through Isaac, this beloved son, God would make a great nation and bless every other nation on earth.

Abraham recounts how he started the journey with Isaac very early the next morning. He did not waste time on worry, fear, or doubt. Many years before, he was committed to obey the voice of God. He had never been sorry, not even once! Every promise had been fulfilled. One step of faith had built upon another. Abraham recited how the Lord shared with him many amazing secrets. Though he lived on earth, Abraham said, "I saw heaven! My heart was always seeking this place. I looked for a city whose builder and maker was God. The Lord showed me my future in visions and dreams. He revealed that Isaac's grandson would lead their family to Egypt and his kin would grow into a mighty nation." God would bring them out with a powerful hand and enrich them as they left. They would be paid an equivalent to four hundred years in back wages when they departed Egypt. He promised to give them the land where Abraham now dwelt. Considering all that the Lord had done. Considering all the promises God made to him concerning Isaac, Abraham believed that even if Isaac died as a sacrifice, the Lord would raise him back to life to fulfill His covenant promise. Abraham knew that nothing was too hard for God. "From the moment I was told to offer Isaac, my heart was set like a flint; to obey the Lord."

This was Abraham's response. Throughout the three days journey, Abraham had a heavy heart. A battle raged in his mind, but his heart was set on obedience. Though our minds try to rob us of faith, if we will focus on the promise Abraham declared, we will overcome in the test of faith. No provision was made for failure. He brought all that was needed for the sacrifice. Abraham even had his son walk up the mountain beside him carrying the wood upon which he would be laid. In Abraham's mind, his son was already dead from the moment he received God's command. Though by faith, he knew Isaac would live again!

Three days' journey with a heavy heart. Three days' journey in a test of faith.

Isaac recounts his experience during those three days noting that his father was unusually quiet. When he asked him about the sacrifice they were about to make, he was a little vague. "Well, at the time," Isaac says, "I thought he was being vague." The truth is, his father spoke prophetically. Isaac saw the wood and the fire for the sacrifice, but they didn't have the lamb—or any animal for that matter—to use as a blood covenant offering. He asked his father about where he would acquire a lamb for the offering. Abraham responded, "God Himself will provide a lamb for an offering."

At the end of those three days on the mountain of Moriah, Abraham built an altar. He laid the wood on the altar that his only beloved son carried there. He bound his son with cords then laid him on the altar. All that was left was to plunge a knife into his son to spill his blood then burn his body on the altar. The Lord God in heaven was watching every step they took. He was weighing the faith and obedience of Abraham. Would he abide by their covenant and give up even to his most precious treasure? The answer was settled on Mount Moriah as Abraham raised his hand to stab his only beloved son in obedience to the command of God. While his hand was raised, the Lord spoke. "Abraham! Abraham!" He said, "Do not slay your son! Now I know that you have fulfilled your covenant promise by faith." In a vision, God shared with Abraham that His only begotten and beloved Son would sacrifice himself on a cross in this very place. He would be the perfect Second Adam who would ultimately pay for the sin of all mankind. He would be a descendant of Abraham and also be the Son of God. Abraham saw that future event in a vision then he understood the blood covenant even more. He rejoiced to see that day! During that three-day journey, Abraham saw the Father's heart and felt some of the Lord's pain and loss. He saw the depth of His love for man and the ultimate sacrifice; that seals the believer's fate.

In heaven's grandstand, the images now appearing are of Mount Moriah, no longer with Isaac on an altar for God Himself provided the lamb. We have returned to the vision of an empty cross standing in that very place. Everyone in the vast assembly of heaven begin to worship the Lamb of God sitting upon the throne, "Worthy is the Lamb to receive glory, praise, and honor! He died and He lives again! Holy is the Lord!"

10

Dream Seeds

Dreams are the seeds
Heaven plants in your heart.
When nurtured, they grow.
A little heaven on earth.

As Abraham and Isaac are seated, another figure rises at the request of the Father. Viewing the multitudes in heaven's grand stadium, we realize there are so many stories to choose from. And all of them glorify God and bring joy to the family.

It is phenomenal to us as observers that there are millions of individuals, glorified saints of all ages, around God's throne, and each one has a story of victory. Throughout eternity, their stories will be told. *Story Time in Heaven* has unlimited story lines, yet God always shows Himself to be strong and powerful in every story. He always brings victory from what looks to be certain defeat. Every person has rich experiences. If each speaker could share with us all that they learned and accomplished in their lives, the tales would go on for eternity. God is at work in all of us all the time. We are never out of His sight, never out of His thoughts, and never out of His presence. Every day; for those who are alert and aware and walk by faith, God is constantly intervening in their lives.

Our next speaker introduces himself as the grandson of Isaac and great-grandson of Abraham. His name is Joseph. The heavenly Father asked him to share a few thoughts from his life concerning the subject of *dreams*. Joseph's narrative begins with a little background about his life. He has ten half brothers. They have the same father (Jacob) but different mothers. Only the youngest, Benjamin, was his brother from both parents. Their mother Rachel was the wife their father loved the most. She died giving birth to Benjamin. Growing up, Joseph shares that his father loved him more than his brothers. He was younger than most of them but he was given favored status by his father. His father even made for him a special multicolored robe! The colors and the beauty of his robe was unrivaled. The favoritism of their father made his brothers resent him greatly. Joseph's relationship with his brothers, except Benjamin, was very strained. Joseph loved his father and his family and worshipped the God of his fathers, the God of Abraham, Isaac, and Jacob. He heard the stories of their blood covenant with the Father God, the creator and preserver of life. He knew about the promises made to Abraham, Isaac, and Jacob and to all their children. He also knew about the dreams where God appeared and spoke to his forefathers. Joseph believed, loved, and followed God.

God began to share dreams with Joseph. The first dream was of him and his eleven brothers working in a field, binding sheaves of grain. Joseph's sheaf arose and stood upright then the other eleven sheaves stood and bowed to his sheaf. Joseph admonishes us not to do what he did when we have a dream. He made the mistake of sharing his dreams with his brothers, which made his brothers hate him. In fact, they did everything in their power to hinder his dream from coming to fruition! Joseph shared a second dream with his family, resulting in even his father's rebuke. In Joseph's second dream, the sun and the moon and the eleven stars were all bowing before him. Jacob asked if he, his mother, and his eleven brothers would come and bow down to him.

Joseph instructs us how important it is to be careful with whom we share our dreams. As a young man, he did not realize that *dreams are fragile things at the start.* He reminded us that *dreams can be lost while still in your heart if not fed with belief and watered with prayer.* He urged us to *be careful with whom you share your dreams because dreams can be destroyed by the doubt of another.* However, regardless of his mistakes, Joseph believed in his God-inspired dreams. He kept them in his heart and meditated on them daily. He continued to do his chores and kept a good attitude. He developed in character and honored his father who loved him so much. His brothers were shepherds and kept the family livestock. Sometimes they would travel quite a distance to find grazing. Joseph stayed at home and did his work and duties near their father.

His father Jacob, whose named was eventually changed to Israel after a unique confrontation with God, instructed Joseph to check on his brothers who were feeding the flock about fifty miles away near Shechem. Israel asked Joseph to see how his brothers and their flocks were doing and to return with word of their status. During that time, it was a few days journey from Hebron where they lived. When he arrived at Shechem, the brothers had already moved on further to pastures in Dothan. Near Dothan, Joseph finally found his brothers.

When they saw Joseph coming from a distance, they were filled with such hatred that they conspired together to destroy him. They called him "the dreamer." They decided to kill him, throw him in a pit, and then tell their father that an animal had devoured him. His brothers then mused, "What would become of the dreamer's big dreams then?" One of the brothers, Reuben, was not comfortable with this plan. He wanted to help Joseph escape. His counsel to his brothers was to cast Joseph into a pit but not to lay a hand upon him so they would not be guilty of murder. His brothers no doubt thought this plan would be even better. He could slowly die alone with only his dreams. A slow, painful, and discouraging death to both Joseph and his dreams. Perfect! When Joseph arrived, they did just that. They tore his multicolored robe right off his back! The beautiful robe their father made was now in tatters. Then they threw him into a pit.

In the throne room of heaven, the three-dimensional hologram is open before us as we hear the story of Joseph. We watch his brothers laughing, scoffing, mocking, and jeering him as Joseph cries out, begging his brothers to help him. We hear their words and feel their hate. They are sitting around a campfire, eating and drinking as

Joseph is without food, water, or even his robe pleading with them and totally at their mercy. They rejoice in his approaching death. Truly, jealousy is cruel as the grave. In the pit below, Joseph appears to be alone. He is exhausted and hungry from his journey. He is disappointed, disillusioned and devastated by the treatment of his brothers. He sees his brothers' hate and anger and is tempted to give in to anger and hate himself. They do not believe in Joseph or his dreams. Being powerless to overcome his brother's strength, a decision confronts Joseph, a choice only he can make. Would he keep on believing in his God-given dreams or would he lose heart and just give up? Joseph decided that God's promise was greater than his brother's hatred. He decided that the God, who made the universe was powerful enough to bring to pass the dream He put in Joseph's heart. In choosing to believe, Joseph learned a powerful lesson in life. *It matters not what others believe. What you believe about your future determines your destiny!*

As his brothers are mocking and laughing above ground, Joseph is in the pit believing in God and in his God-given dream. In the distance, a caravan of traders is approaching their camp. One of the brothers is inspired with an even more evil and sinister idea. This will certainly destroy Joseph's dream. "Let's sell him as a slave to these traders! The traders are on their way to Egypt!" They discuss how they will make some money and get rid of Joseph at the same time. Even better, they will reverse his dream into a nightmare. Instead of people bowing to him, Joseph will be a slave. He will be bowing to everyone else. "*Haha!* This is too sweet!" they said. Joseph is hauled up from the pit, bound like a slave. His every possession, including the beautiful coat his father made with such love, is taken from him. Joseph begs them for mercy. He implores them to let him go free, but they mock him and carry out their evil plan. Joseph is sold by his own brothers for a few pieces of silver. Now they believe he will never be a ruler, but he will be ruled by others for the rest of his life! Joseph has absolutely nothing left—except his dream.

Dreams all seem to die before they come true. It is simply the nature of dreams. There's a birth, then a death, then a resurrection, it seems.

On the long, dusty road to Egypt, Joseph treks. He is forced to walk, serve, and obey people he doesn't even know. This loved son is worse than a servant, he is a slave. Joseph is expected to obey the commands of others. "At that time," Joseph explains, "there were many slaves of all races all over the world. When one country conquered another, they would murder most of the men. The conquering army would then enslave the rest of the population—men, women, and children."

Mankind had degraded far from what God created perfectly in the garden of Eden with Adam. But Joseph had an uncommon understanding about life. When so many others fought against the bonds, commands, and constraints of others; when so many let bitterness, anger, and hatred invade their souls and poison their minds, Joseph understood a principle, shared generations later in a special message called, the Sermon on the Mount. As Joseph shares this principle, he looks at the Son of God seated on the right hand of the Father of Love, and smiles. The principle is the law of the second mile, which goes, when compelled to go a mile, make it two. Why on earth would Joseph do that? Joseph understood that when you move beyond what is required and do much more, you move into the realm of choice. At that point the weight and bitterness of the command has lost its power over your mind and heart. Instead of being required to do a service, you *choose* to do a service and to do it in *excellence*. You are changed from a servant to a master of your own destiny. What magnifies its power even more is when you make this decision, you commit to do everything to honor God.

Joseph decided early on the journey to Egypt that he would live by the law of the second mile. He believed he would rule one day. He believed God had a purpose and a destiny for him. He was determined to be the best at whatever he did. Joseph did not waste his time in unforgiveness and hatred for his brothers back home. No time was wasted in anger or resentment toward those he was forced to serve. He had the seed of a dream germinating in his heart, which would bring greatness up ahead.

When dreams seem to die in the outside world,
they are still planted deep in your heart.
Your dreams are germinating, simply sending
down roots to support their great size!

Upon arriving in Egypt, Joseph was sold to a very important man named Potiphar. Potiphar was an officer of Pharaoh, the ruler of Egypt. He is the captain of the guard. In the hologram, we are traveling with Joseph to the land of Egypt. This ancient land along the Nile River is beautiful. The homes of the ruler and his officials are very comfortable. In fact, they're luxurious! Joseph had never seen anything like that before! As he began serving Potiphar with respect and honor, he took his duties very seriously. Joseph did his work in excellence. Everything he was asked to do, he did from his heart with pride and purpose to benefit his master. Somehow he knew that as he served others, he was really serving God. Potiphar noticed that everything Joseph did, the Lord prospered. He could see the favor of God upon Joseph's life. This pleased Potiphar. Joseph found grace in his sight and he served him well. He was eventually so confident in Joseph and his abilities that Potiphar made him the overseer of his entire household. Everyone else who worked for Potiphar now worked for Joseph. In just a short time, because of his attitude, Joseph's dream led him from a servant to a ruler in Potiphar's house.

Joseph learned so much in this time at Potiphar's house. He learned that *dreams change your attitude and outlook on life. The present challenge becomes a passing moment, not a permanent place.* As he ruled Potiphar's house, Joseph learned much about life in Egypt. He was no longer bound by ropes or chains. He wore fine clothes. He learned the Egyptian language. He walked the streets, interacting with others, seeing the sights, purchasing supplies, and running all the affairs of the house. Everything in the household was Joseph's responsibility. Potiphar concerned himself with nothing but the food he ate. Potiphar was a soldier. He understood authority. He understood the chain of command. He served Pharaoh well, and Joseph served him. Potiphar delegated authority, trust, and responsibility to Joseph of all that he possessed. Joseph was a good man. He found favor with all the Egyptians around him. He was a man well-respected. Though on the outside, Joseph had been a slave, he was never a slave in his heart. In his heart, he was always a leader, a ruler of men. That was the dream God gave him. That was what Joseph believed!

11

Believe in Your Dreams

Closed doors are never the end that they seem,
But simply a turning point on the way to your dream!

In heaven, the hologram disappears for a short time as the saints of all ages contemplate the adventure we are witnessing. Joseph has moved from the pit to a place of leadership and authority in just a few short years. We rejoice in his victory. We rejoice in the favor of God upon his life. We rejoice in the power of a promise (a dream), a word from God. Every word God has ever spoken is alive! It contains the power to produce what it proclaims for those who will mix the promise with faith.

God's words are seeds of all that will be!

During this imaginary journey to heaven, we have also observed that even as we relive the stories, the heavenly Father is constantly engaged with every searching soul. As *Story Time in Heaven* is broadcasting before us on the gigantic hologram, we also observe that requests are received constantly before His throne of grace. Our Father God is not distracted by these requests. While we focus on one or two things at a time, He is focused on all things at once. There is constant activity before the throne. People are always approaching the throne boldly in the spirit. These individuals are not yet citizens of heaven, but believers on earth by the thousands. They approach in spirit and in faith. Some are approaching individually, some approach in groups. They do not see what we are seeing now in heaven; but from earth. They are reaching into heaven through prayer. These prayers remain before the throne within the golden vase. The sweet aroma they emit filled with praise, worship, trust, and desire for divine intervention is precious to the Father and the Son.

The Son of God is forever interceding before the Father. As the requests arrive, the Son acknowledges those who believe. He is their advocate, their representative, and their defense attorney in heaven. Jesus, our Savior, gestures to the scarlet liquid flowing over the golden covenant container and the golden covering of winged angels above it upon which the scarlet liquid flows. He refers to it as the "mercy seat." As the Son acknowledges those who come in faith, the Father of love grants their requests. No packages are sent, no shipment is made. The answer given is a word! It is a "yes" to the promise in answer to the request. Believing in the promise sent from heaven explodes in provision on earth. This occurs when the promise is combined with faith in the hearts of those who receive. We are informed that on earth there must be an "Amen" or "so be it" by faith, from the lips and heart of believers to activate their miracle. Grace (God's unmerited favor) and mercy is flowing freely, constantly, and in unlimited supply from the throne of God. It is received by all who seek His face in faith.

The power of God's word mixed with faith in the heart of a believer is more powerful than any chemical or atomic reaction on earth! Spiritual power is far greater than natural power.

The vastness of heaven's stadium, the constant activity before the throne, and the dynamic and exciting adventures of faith displayed on the hologram of heaven simply astounds us! Prior to taking this imaginary journey, we had no idea how incredible heaven would be! Not only is the throne room so magnificent, but so are the city, the mansions, the streets, and the citizens of heaven! Additionally, to be in the presence of the God, whose very essence is *love*, fills us with such awe. Never have we felt anything so rich, so deep, and so all-encompassing as the *love* of God! As we are enjoying this glorious encounter, there is much more to be revealed of eternity in God's world beyond what we have seen this far. Our hearts race with anticipation and joy!

Joseph rises to his feet again. All eyes turn to him. Then as the hologram appears, we see the young and successful overseer of Potiphar's household. He carries on his duties and responsibilities with such kindness and skill. Under Joseph's leadership, prosperity abounds. Potiphar's servants are skilled and do their work with professionalism. The assets of his master grow daily. Truly, the favor of God us upon Potiphar because of the presence and leadership of Joseph. Joseph is a very handsome and intelligent man. No longer a boy, he has matured and developed into a very impressive individual in stature, knowledge, and respect. Potiphar has a wife who is now taking notice of their overseer. She begins to desire Joseph rather than her husband. Lust develops in her heart. She first tries to seduce and entice him with her beauty and charm. She acts in a flirtatious and sensuous manner. As he rejects her advances respectfully, Potiphar's wife becomes more demanding. She wants him to come to her bed, sleep with her, and fulfill her sensual desires. Joseph is firm in his loyalty to Potiphar. He tells her straightforwardly that he will not betray her husband. Joseph reminds her that Potiphar put him in charge over everything in his household. The only thing that he has not given to Joseph is his wife. Joseph is emphatic that it would be evil and wicked to meet her demands and sleep with her. He added that it would be a sin against God!

Daily, Potiphar's wife continued to pursue Joseph. She became obsessed with the desire for his affections. The more he resisted her advances, the more she desired the conquest! Even though Joseph tried to avoid contact with her, some of his duties required him to enter the house to do his master's business. One day when there were no other men in the house, Joseph came in to work. Potiphar's wife, in a fit of lustful desire, grabbed him by his garments. She demanded that he come to her bed and lay with her to fulfill her desires and demands. Joseph broke free, left his garment in her hand and fled quickly, exiting the house. From this rejection, her lust turned to a deep hatred. Seeing the garment in her hand, Potiphar's wife screamed to alert the men of the house who had been outside at the time. She falsely accused Joseph of trying to rape her. She lied that Joseph fled and left his garment with her when she resisted him and cried out for help. Potiphar's wife saved Joseph's garment beside her until her husband came home that evening. When he arrived, she then began to spin a lie about Joseph and attacked his character. She falsely declared that he mocked her, acted in a lewd manner to her, and aggressively tried to enter her bedchamber to rape her. She presented the evidence of Joseph's garment, which her husband recognized. She said Joseph left it when he fled her room. Her loud cry for help was all that saved her from defilement, making Joseph run in panic. She then accused her husband of not protecting her by bringing the Hebrew servant to their home.

This put Potiphar on the defensive. After hearing his wife's accusations, Potiphar was angry. Joseph's master put him into the prison. He was placed in a very secure part of the prison where the king's prisoners were bound. Joseph had no trial. He had no recourse. His dream, it seems, had come to a crashing end. The door that had been opened for him to rise in leadership and power was now closed, just like the door to his jail cell had crashed loudly behind him. Through no fault of his own, Joseph was utterly destitute again. He had nothing. His fine clothing was changed to prison garments. He was now worse than a slave. Joseph was a prisoner with nothing—but his *dreams.*

Dreams are beautiful things
because they really can change the scene!

In jail, Joseph was again faced with a decision. He could allow bitterness and resentment to embrace his mind and heart and destroy his life. He could blame his misfortune on others, on circumstances, or—as some do—blame it all on God. However, Joseph's knowledge and experience would not allow him to do so. Complaining, becoming bitter, bearing unforgiveness or hatred—all of these are poison to a dreamer. When you have a dream in your heart, you embrace it in faith. When God puts a dream in your heart, He plants a seed in your soul! Weeds of bitterness, doubt, unforgiveness, hatred, or lust will squeeze the life out of your dream seeds before they ever mature. Weeding the garden of dreams in your heart is as important as feeding your dreams with faith and watering them with prayer.

Though Joseph was a prisoner in his body, he was a free man and a dreamer in his soul. In his mind and heart, prison was but a step toward his dream, the ultimate goal. He was determined to be the best he could be wherever he was planted. Just as a servant in Potiphar's house he rose to rule the house, so as a prisoner in the king's prison he will rise to rule over all. Many people dream but some do not believe in their dreams. For them, they are really just wishes, not dreams. Joseph believed and acted upon his dreams.

Many people dream, fewer believe.
Dreaming is enjoyable. Believing is powerful!

As Joseph interacted with the keeper of the prison and the other prisoners, the Lord was with Joseph. God's favor was upon him. The keeper of the prison started giving Joseph responsibilities, which Joseph fulfilled in excellence. Joseph proved himself trustworthy. More and more responsibility came his way until, again, the prisoner became the ruler. Eventually, the keeper of the prison committed all the prisoners to Joseph's care. The keeper of the prison was completely comfortable and confident in Joseph's character and skill. He simply delegated all authority to Joseph, recognizing that the Lord was with him in all that he did.

Joseph reminds us, "Your gift will make room for you wherever you go! Keep developing your God-given gifts even when it looks futile." The Lord made everything Joseph put his hand on prosper. The prisoner now ruled the prison! Joseph held the keys to everyone's cells. How the scene can change if you just believe in God-given dreams!

It had been over a decade now that Joseph was in Egypt. He had become very familiar with the Egyptian people and their ways.

Yet Joseph continued to be faithful to the God of his fathers. He continued to believe in his dreams. After several years in prison, two new arrivals entered the prison together. Both were servants to the pharaoh, one was his butler and the other his baker. Somehow they had both offended the king that day. The pharaoh was angry with the chief of the butlers and the chief of the bakers. These two were placed in the section of the prison where Joseph had authority. The captain of the guard charged Joseph with the responsibility of caring for them, and he served them. After a season in the prison, they both had a dream on the same night. The next morning, Joseph was making his rounds in the prison.

As observers of this story in heaven, we all smile as we see Joseph walking about freely within the prison and holding the keys. As Joseph is recounting the story as it appears on the hologram, we are all amazed that no matter the circumstance, the Favor of God shows up.

As he came to where the butler and baker are held, Joseph noticed a sadness about them. Joseph inquired about their sadness as he was charged with their care. The officers recounted how they had each had a dream. They felt the dreams had significance but knew no one who could interpret them. Joseph responded that interpretations of dreams belongs to God and asked them to share the dream with him. The butler told Joseph that in his dream, there was a vine with three branches. The vine budded, blossomed and brought forth grapes. In the dream, the pharaoh's cup was in the butler's hand. He took the grapes, pressed them into the cup, and passed the cup to the Pharaoh's hand.

God gave Joseph the interpretation. "The three branches are three days," Joseph said. "Within three days, the pharaoh will restore you to your place and you will deliver Pharaoh's cup into his hand, just as you always did before as his butler." Joseph went on to ask the butler, "When you are back in your position, please remember me. Make mention of me to the pharaoh and bring me out of this prison. I was stolen away out of my homeland and I have done nothing to deserve this place!"

Seeing the interpretation was favorable for the butler, the baker also informed Joseph of his dream. "In my dream, I had three white baskets on my head. In the top basket were all kinds of baked goods for Pharaoh, but the birds ate them out of the basket on my head," he shared. God gave Joseph this interpretation also. He sadly informed the baker that the three baskets are three days. Within three days, the pharaoh will behead him and hang him on a tree. The birds would eat his flesh.

Three days later, it was the pharaoh's birthday and he provided a feast for all his servants. At the dinner table, he restored the chief butler to his position and he gave the cup into Pharaoh's hand, but the pharaoh hanged the chief baker, just as Joseph interpreted their dreams. Sadly, the chief butler did not remember Joseph. Two more long years passed, Joseph continued to dream. After two years of waiting and over a decade of service, this young man matured physically, developed mentally, grew spiritually, and displayed solid character. His dreams remained intact, his heart remained steadfast, and his faith and wisdom grew. At the appointed time, he was ready for all that now follows.

In the palace, Pharaoh dreamed that out of the Nile came seven cows, fat and robust in health. In his dream, he stood by watching these cows grazing among the reeds. After them, seven other cows, ugly and thin, came up out of the Nile and stood beside the first cows on the riverbank. The thin cows then ate the fat and robust cows. Then Pharaoh woke up. When he fell back asleep, he had a second dream. Seven heads of grain, healthy and good, were growing on a single stalk. After them, seven other heads of grain sprouted, thin and scorched by the east wind. The thin heads of grain swallowed up the seven healthy ones. Then Pharaoh awakened again. In the morning, he was troubled by the dreams and felt there was a deep meaning to them. Pharaoh called for the wisest men in his land to see who could understand his dream. No one was found with wisdom that could interpret these dreams. At this point, the butler, Pharaoh's cupbearer, was reminded of Joseph. He told the king the story of how Joseph interpreted both his dream and the baker's with accuracy in prison two years ago. He informed the king about the details of their dreams and Joseph's interpretation. Pharaoh sent for Joseph immediately.

He was quickly brought up from the dungeon. After he had shaved and changed his clothes, Joseph was ushered into Pharaoh's presence. He told Joseph that he dreamed something significant the night before but did not know the interpretation of the dream. Pharaoh told Joseph that he was aware Joseph could interpret dreams. Joseph was quick to declare that he did not have that power, but the God who he served would give Pharaoh the answer to his dreams. Pharaoh then recited his dream of the seven cows and the seven heads of grain.

God revealed the interpretation to Joseph and Joseph told its interpretation to Pharaoh. Both dreams dealt with the same subject. They are really one dream, not two. The reason God gave it in two different ways was to emphasize the importance and surety of the dream. God was revealing to Pharaoh what He was about to do. He said that the first seven fat cows and the seven healthy heads of grain represented seven years of abundance that are coming for the land of Egypt. The seven ugly cows and the seven scorched heads of grain represented seven years of famine to follow. Joseph then instructed the pharaoh to look for a wise and discerning man to put in the charge of the land of Egypt. He should appoint commissioners over the land who will take twenty percent of all the food during the good years that are coming and store up the grain under his authority. These are to be kept and preserved for the seven years of famine that will follow so that the nation of Egypt will survive and not be destroyed by the famine.

This plan met with Pharaoh's approval and the approval of all his officials. He told his officials that in all of Egypt, there was no one as wise as Joseph who stood before him now since God had revealed His plan to him. He assigned Joseph to take charge of his palace and declared that his people were to submit to Joseph's orders and instructions. Only Pharaoh himself would be greater than Joseph as he was declared to be overseer of the entire land of Egypt! The king put his signet ring, the symbol of his authority, on Joseph's finger. He put fine linen on him, robes of royalty, and placed a gold chain about his neck. Joseph rode in a chariot as the pharaoh's second-in-command in all of Egypt. He was told by Pharaoh that no one will lift a hand or foot in all the land of Egypt without Joseph's word. When Joseph entered the pharaoh's service, he was thirty years old.

God uses dreams to help you create a world that is better tomorrow.

12

Dreams Change Your World

Dreams open our earthly world to heavenly ideas!

As we listen to Joseph's story here in heaven, our hearts smile within us. We are seeing before our very eyes the realization of a lifelong dream. We are also seeing the fulfilment of prophetic words spoken to Abraham, the friend of God. Abraham was told that in his great-grandson's generation, his family would move to Egypt. We are also seeing the value of believing in God-given dreams and visions in vivid color. We have much more to learn from Joseph as he continues the adventure.

During his years of service to Potiphar and later in prison, Joseph learned to depend upon God for everything. He learned how to lead others. He spoke the language fluently. He could converse with everyone from prisoner and servant, to business leaders, and those with authority and leadership in the land. He learned how to listen to the voice of God. He learned how to dream and to achieve. All the skills he acquired while under the pressure of difficult circumstances prepared him for what was ahead.

As the second-in-command of the entire nation of Egypt, Joseph now had immense responsibility. To prepare for the challenge facing the nation, Joseph, as a first step, traveled to every part of the country. He took stock of its assets. He examined their storage facilities and assessed their needs for the coming drought. God had informed Joseph (and the pharaoh through Joseph) that wise planning was necessary. Because Joseph could dream, he could see and plan for events with great skill. As he looked at the challenges and meditated upon the situation, God gave him inspired ideas. He was given heavenly answers for earthly problems. Joseph initiated the construction of storage facilities in every Egyptian city. He informed the citizens in each area of the upcoming challenges. He enlisted their help in preparing for the drought. He commanded that all Egyptians bring twenty percent of all their crops to these locations. Because the first seven years of abundance were so great, huge amounts of harvested grain were placed in the storage buildings. Very soon, every city had massive warehouse facilities constructed and filled with produce from the surrounding fields. As the harvests came in during the first seven years, they were all filled. The harvest of grain and corn was so plentiful that Joseph could no longer count the volume. There was so much corn that it was like the sands of the sea!

Pharaoh changed Joseph's name when he placed him over Egypt to Zaphnath-paaneah. He was also given a wife named Asenath, the daughter of Potipherah, a priest of On. During the seven years of abundance, Joseph had an amazing life. Two sons were born to his wife. Manasseh was his firstborn. Joseph said as he named him, "God hath made me forget all my toil, and all my father's house" (Gen. 41:51, ASV). His second son, Joseph named Ephraim, "God hath caused me to be fruitful in the land of my affliction" (Gen. 41:52, KJV). As Joseph enjoyed these years of plenty with his wife and family, he also wondered about his father and brothers and what had become of them.

At this point in the story, another figure stands beside Joseph. He introduces himself to the assembly of saints as Jacob or Israel, the father of Joseph. His son yields the floor to his father as Israel begins to recount what happened years before when his son went missing. He had sent Joseph to check on his brothers and their flocks. After many days when they returned, his brothers brought the multicolored coat he made for his son. It was torn and covered in blood! The brothers asked if he knew this coat and of course he did. It was Joseph's coat! Jacob was immediately certain that Joseph must have been killed by a wild animal. His heart broke and he grieved for a very long time. He loved Joseph so much. He was the first child of his beloved wife Rachel. His heart ached for this fine son who was so kind, so wise, so intelligent, and so loving. Israel went on to share the sadness that seemed to grip him after the loss of Joseph. He clung even more closely to Joseph's younger brother, Benjamin. One son was all that he had left of his beloved Rachel. Israel speaks. "About twenty years after we lost Joseph, a severe famine gripped our land. It was extremely difficult to find forage for our animals as we were shepherds. It was challenging to find food for my children and grandchildren."

Joseph then speaks again about what happened in Egypt. "The seven years of plenty ended. A severe famine began in the land. It was not only in Egypt, but in all the surrounding countries as well! When all the people in Egypt were hungry, they cried out to Pharaoh for bread. Pharaoh's response to all of them was, 'Go to Joseph and what he says, do'." Joseph opened the storehouses in each city and sold supplies and corn to the Egyptians. Because the famine was so great over the entire area, people from other countries also came to Egypt to buy corn. All authorization for the sale of corn or supplies was required to go through Joseph. Without his approval, no one could purchase anything under the pharaoh's control.

Jacob then interjects that he had heard from others in their land of Canaan that there was corn in Egypt. He sent all of his sons, except Benjamin, to the land of Egypt to buy corn for their families. Israel did not send Benjamin for fear something might happen to him on the journey. His other ten sons arrived in Egypt.

Joseph recounts that he was then the governor of Egypt. It was his responsibility to watch over and disperse the supplies. All who came to purchase food must come to him, whether Egyptian or foreigner. Joseph's brothers came. They bowed down before Joseph with their faces to the earth. When Joseph saw his brothers, he knew them and remembered his very first dream. It was now being fulfilled! It was surprising, breathtaking, and satisfying. Joseph was dressed like an Egyptian. He disguised himself to them. He talked to them roughly through an interpreter. He knew his brothers, but they did not know him. Joseph accused his brothers of being spies. He accused them of coming at a vulnerable time for their nation (during a severe drought) to prepare to steal from or to overpower the land. His brothers denied the charges. They informed Joseph that they were just there to buy food. They insisted they were all brothers, sons of the same father, and that they were not spies. They told more about their family as Joseph pressed them for information. They informed Joseph that there were originally twelve sons. "One, our youngest brother, is with our father and one is dead."

Joseph insisted they were spies. Finally, he informed his brothers that they could not leave unless the youngest brother was brought to him. He told the brothers to pick one of their number to go home and get their younger brother and the rest would be held in prison until they both returned. For three days, the brothers were held in prison. On the third day, Joseph called for the brothers to be brought to him. He had another idea. They were to pick one of the brothers to stay and the rest would go home to bring their younger brother back with them. He was testing the veracity of their words. His brothers began discussing the guilt they all felt for what they did to Joseph so many years earlier. They had seen the anguish of his soul when he begged them not to sell him and they turned a deaf ear. They discussed how this problem facing them was no doubt because of their wicked treatment of Joseph. Reuben emphasized how he instructed them not to sin against Joseph, but they would not listen. "Now his blood is on our hands!"

His brothers did not know he was Joseph or that he understood what they were saying. Joseph was overwhelmed with emotion. He turned away from his brothers and wept. Once he regained his composure, Joseph continued talking through an interpreter. It was decided that Simeon would be held in jail until the rest of them returned with their youngest brother. He took Simeon, bound him before their eyes, and then sent them away. Joseph commanded their sacks be filled with corn and that everyone's money was put back in his sack. They loaded their pack animals with the corn and departed from Egypt. Along the way, they stopped at an inn. When one of the brothers opened his sack to feed his animals, he saw all his money at the top of the sack. They were immediately afraid.

Jacob picks up the story here. He informs us of how disturbed and upset the brothers were when they arrived back in Canaan. All of them still had their money when their sacks were opened. They told the whole account of the journey about the governor of the land and the way he accused them of being spies. They also said that Simeon was left there in prison. They could not return for any more provisions unless Benjamin came along with them. Jacob told his sons that he would never allow them to take Benjamin with them to Egypt. "If something happened to him on the way," Jacob said, "you will bring down my gray hairs with sorrow to the grave!" They all stayed home until the supplies were almost completely exhausted.

When Jacob was given notice that the supply of corn was depleted, he instructed his sons to go to Egypt again and buy food for their families. Judah responded that the governor of the land was very emphatic that we would not see his face again unless they bring Benjamin with them. He assured his father that they would return only if Benjamin accompanied them on the journey. Israel was frustrated with his sons and scolded them for saying they had another brother. The brothers said that the governor asked them specifically about their family. "He asked if our father was alive. He asked us if we had any other brothers. We answered the man truthfully, not knowing he would instruct us to bring our youngest brother to Egypt." Judah promised his father Israel that he would guarantee Benjamin's safe return. "If we had not lingered until so late a time when our food is gone, we could have been there and back again already!" he said.

Israel told them to take the best fruits of the land and bring them as a present to the governor of Egypt. "Take a little balm, some honey, spices, myrrh, nuts, and almonds. Take double the money that was back in your sacks. Perhaps it was returned as an oversight. Also, Benjamin may accompany you to the man". He prayed that God Almighty would give them mercy and that they would return not just with Benjamin, but with Simeon also. They gathered everything their father had instructed them to take, along with Benjamin, journeying back to Egypt...and stood before Joseph.

Joseph continues the adventure. When he saw his brother Benjamin with them, Joseph was pleased. In his heart, he had longed to see Benjamin for many years. He gave notice to the ruler of his house to slay an animal and make dinner ready because these men will dine with him at noon. His brothers were brought to Joseph's magnificent home. The second-in-command of Egypt had servants and many buildings in his compound. It was second in beauty only to the pharaoh's palace. There were carvings and tapestries, stables for horses and a place for his chariot, and large rooms and hallways that led to the dining area. Joseph's brothers were afraid that this may be a setup because of the money in their sacks the last time. Joseph was going to enslave them and take all their animals and supplies. They discussed with the steward of Joseph's house about what happened the last time they were there and how when they opened their sacks at an inn on the journey home, all their money was still inside. They said they had brought the money back plus more to purchase supplies for this trip. The steward comforted them and told them not to fear because their God and the God of their father gave the treasure in their sacks. He also brought Simeon out to them. The brothers were given water to wash their feet and provisions for their animals. They gazed in awe at the home's magnificence.

In the dining room, one long table was set up for eleven and another separate table higher than the long table, forming a T at the head of the hall. They prepared to have lunch with Joseph. They also brought in the gifts their father sent along for him. When Joseph arrived, they bowed themselves to the earth, all eleven brothers, and gave Joseph the gifts. They discussed their trip home. Joseph asked about their father. Was he well? The brothers responded that all were well, including their father. Then they all bowed down their heads and made obeisance. Joseph thought how accurate was the dream of his youth! Joseph then noticed Benjamin, his mother's son. He inquired if this was their younger brother they had spoken about. He spoke a blessing over Benjamin, saying, "May God be gracious unto you!"

At this point, Joseph was so overwhelmed with love and longing to embrace his brother that he left the room for a few minutes. He went into his bedchamber to weep tears of joy. When his composure returned, Joseph washed his face, left his room to rejoin his brothers, and then commanded his servants to set the table for dinner. Joseph ate at the head table by himself because it was an abomination, for Egyptians to eat bread with Hebrews. Joseph had them seated in order of age with Benjamin closest to Joseph's table. The brothers marveled how they had been seated so accurately in order of age. Huge amounts of food and drink filled the banquet table. Joseph's servants placed large portions in front of everyone. None of the brothers had ever been entertained with such lavishness. However, Benjamin's portion was five times larger than the rest of the brothers. They all ate, drank, and had wonderful conversation together. There was great joy in the dining hall that day! Joseph's brothers spent the night. Joseph then commanded his steward to fill every sack completely with corn, place their money back in the mouth of their sacks, and then place his personal silver goblet in Benjamin's sack. In the morning, the men were sent away with all their possessions and supplies.

Once the brothers were out of the city, not far down the road, Joseph instructed his steward to follow them and overtake them. When he caught them, he was to ask why they had rewarded evil for good. "Why have you stolen my master's silver goblet?" The brothers reacted with shock and surprise. They reminded the steward that they had brought double the money back from the last excursion to their land. "Why would we then steal silver or gold from your master? If you find the silver goblet, let the one who has it be killed and the rest of us will be your slaves!" The steward agreed that whoever was found to have it in their possession would be his slave and the rest would go away blameless. A search was made of all their sacks beginning with the oldest to the youngest. The silver goblet was found in Benjamin's sack. All of them were devastated by this discovery. They tore their clothes in anguish and headed back to Joseph's house with all their possessions. When they came before Joseph, he reprimanded them. He told them that he could divine what they were doing. Judah interceded. He said that they would be his servants, but Joseph required only Benjamin, the one in whose sack the goblet was found. Judah continued to intercede. He talked about Joseph being dead and how Benjamin was the only one left of Rachel's children.

He informed Joseph of Jacob's words, and how he did not want to send Benjamin but he vouched for the boy. Judah asked to become a slave in his brother's stead. He did not want to bring grief and death to their father by the loss of Benjamin.

At this point, Joseph could no longer restrain himself. He began to weep uncontrollably! He commanded all his attendants to leave him alone with these men. Then Joseph revealed himself to his brothers. He said, "I am Joseph!" They were shocked and trembled in fear, afraid he was angry. Joseph went on to recount his journey to Egypt, his appointment to second in authority to the pharaoh alone. He encouraged them by saying that though they had sent him away with evil intent, God had been the one who led him to Egypt. He had been sent ahead to preserve their entire family. Joseph also informed his brothers that the famine was only in its second year. Pharaoh's dream indicated that the famine would last for five more years. He comforted his brothers. He wept on Benjamin's shoulder and Benjamin wept on his as they embraced. All the brothers then embraced Joseph in love, in healing, in forgiveness, and in thanksgiving.

When word came to Pharaoh that Joseph's brothers had arrived, he was very pleased. He loved and appreciated Joseph, as did everyone in Egypt. He told Joseph to send his brothers home with gifts and supplies and to return to Egypt with their father and the rest of their family. They were sent away with wagons filled with supplies. "When you return," the pharaoh said, "I will give you the good of the land of Egypt, and you shall eat the fat of the land!"

Arriving at home, Jacob did not believe their story about Joseph at first. But when he saw the wagons and heard the exciting and miraculous account of God's provision from his sons, his heart was encouraged. Israel said, "Joseph my son is still alive! I will go and see him before I die!" When they all arrived in Egypt, Joseph and his father embraced. Their hearts found healing and great joy. Pharaoh, the king, came to greet them. He said that the best of the land was available for them. Israel and his sons were asked where they would like to settle. Joseph had instructed them to ask for the land of Goshen because it was the most fertile land and great for grazing their animals. Pharaoh gave them Goshen, and they enjoyed plenty while the famine surrounded them. God had used Joseph's dreams, his obedience, and his faithfulness to turn something that was intended by others for evil into something very good in his life, his family's life, and for the entire nation of Egypt!

Dreams are the seeds heaven plants in your heart. When nurtured, they grow. A little Heaven on earth!

All of heaven's assembly rejoices with Joseph and his family. We just witnessed the story, saw the action, felt their emotions, and now embrace their victory. The final frame of a wonderful family of approximately seventy people rejoicing in Goshen fades with the hologram. We are again in the spirit of our imagination, beholding the joy of heaven's great family and the Father they so love. We rejoice in the power of faith. God-given words and dreams bring such blessing to so many. God-given dreams don't just bless the dreamer, they also bless and touch the lives of others. We rejoice in the power of forgiveness that frees from guilt and bitterness and heals relationships, elevating them to a higher and deeper level. Faith, love, and forgiveness—these are the common attributes that flow in heaven's family. As we look around heaven's stadium, we see Joseph, his father Israel, his grandfather Isaac, and his great-grandfather Abraham. They are rejoicing together. We remember the prophecies shared by God with his friend Abraham of all that had happened and of even greater things yet to come for his family.

In this segment of the family's story, the dreamer's dreams came to life! As we observe Joseph's story during this imaginary visit to heaven, we are reminded to: *speak your dreams, not your doubts. Speak your faith, not your fears. What you give voice to, you give power to in your life!*

The Father of Love now imparts new revelation, some important truths to our spirits that are highlighted in the family history to this point. He informs us that dreams are an important trait that He placed in the family from the very beginning. He, the Father of Light, the Creator had a dream of creating a family that would reflect His glory, grace, and love. We are created in His image and just as

His dreams and words have power, our dreams and words have power as well. In the garden of Eden, Adam dreamed, thought, and envisioned how he desired the garden to look and he released his dreams and desires through words. The plant and animal life responded to his direction. When he maintained his dreams in accordance with the Father's overall direction and purpose, wonderful beauty resulted. However, whenever his dreams took him away from the Father's direction, disaster ensued! *Some dream great dreams, others devise evil schemes. Thoughts first took them there.*

13

Second Intermission

No matter how much we see, there is more yet to see.
No matter how much we know, there is more yet to know.

During this illuminating and fantastic adventure to heaven, we are hearing incredible stories, learning important truths, and discovering that there is so much more to life than a few short years on earth. We have been guided in our imaginary journey by the spirit who reveals to each of us some of the amazing experiences and places God prepared for those who love Him. We pause in a heavenly intermission. *Story Time in Heaven* will resume soon. As we are awaiting, the next legendary saga, we are left to contemplate, hear, meditate, and be led deeper into the beauty of God's eternity.

In my imagination, I have come to know that on this first imaginary journey to heaven, several more important citizens of this majestic city will enlighten us with their adventures. These individuals will recite significant parts of their journey on earth, all focused around one overriding truth. Their experiences on earth will expand upon and add real color and depth to this most significant of truths as it ties the beginning, the end, and all points in between with a scarlet thread. This scarlet thread of blood covenant relationship runs through all the sacred scriptures. The Father of love has chosen these particular accounts for us at this time. He sees us here and knows our thoughts and imaginations as He knows all things. Our Father desires that we know the truths that will be shared during this imaginary visit to heaven. I have also come to know in my heart that we will be making more than one excursion to heaven. On additional trips, detailed in succeeding accounts, we will be introduced to more dynamic citizens of heaven and, through them, to numerous, exciting, and eternal truths. We will also traverse to areas in eternity that we have not seen or heard a whisper about in our travels thus far. We will see much more of the heavenly city where the translated saints from earth dwell in fantastic mansions. We will also see beyond the city into many other areas of eternity.

Outside the heavenly city are realms about which we have heard references, while walking on earth. They were spoken of by holy men of old, individuals who were inspired by the Spirit of God. One of these areas contains a throne room completely different than the throne in heaven's grandstand. This is a throne of judgment, not a throne of grace. At the center of this room is a gigantic, pure white throne. In this section of eternity, we will find the location of an expansive library far larger than any library on earth. Contained within are trillions of volumes of full video, audio, and written records. These accounts can be projected on another giant hologram. Recorded within them are the detailed actions, down to every idle word, ever spoken by individuals on earth. These are the records of those who did not receive or acknowledge the Father of love. These records are of those who are not in the city of heaven. These are very different stories when contrasted to the epic accounts that we are hearing on this adventure. The narratives recounted before the white throne are sad with tragic endings. We would call these disturbing accounts the horror stories of eternity. A great distance away is another area of severe suffering, a place no one ever wants to go. Though made by our loving heavenly Father, it was not originally made for man to experience, but for an entirely different species of beings. We will learn about these other beings who are led by the invader who seduced Eve in the garden. We will learn of their interaction with man and their effect upon mankind. This journey will involve the war stories of heaven but these accounts are reserved for future imaginary adventures to *Story Time in Heaven*. So much yet to learn, so much more to know. We all feel great anticipation for the upcoming adventures in eternity and the rest of our first imaginary tour of heaven.

In the throne room of heaven, so much is going on around us. Across the glassy sea forming the floor of heaven's stadium and on all levels of the grandstand of this glorious stadium, millions of saints are sharing individual stories. They are answering questions and sharing experiences and the love of heaven's family with others. The language of the spirit is flowing between them. It amazes me how fluent everyone is in this heavenly language. They find no need for an interpreter because of one powerful fact. No matter what period they lived in or what language they spoke on earth, the effect of what God did when he confused men's languages at the tower of Babel is suspended when we get to heaven. Each one converses freely with all those around them. Each has a connection of love in the spirit that is deep, powerful, and eternal. They recognize each other not by earthly traits or earthly ties, but by a bond stronger than any earthly connection. This bond is the blood tie of heaven's family that all in this celestial city share. Each one is a child of God, therefore everyone is a brother or sister. We are hearing stories from saints of God from all ages of time. We listen in as ministers, missionaries, teachers, friends, and family members we knew or heard stories about on earth recount their journey and their joy here in heaven. I see saints of God I have admired and inspired me. Their stories all have one theme in common, they glorify God.

Before the next speaker shares his story with the family of God from heaven's podium, we hear a trumpet sound. At this signal, the orchestra comprised of every musical instrument known on earth, begins releasing a heavenly and harmonic sound. Though I loved music on earth, I must admit some of the instruments in heaven with very unique and peculiar sounds, I have never seen, heard, or recognized on earth. It is so difficult to describe the variations of sound and the depth of harmony and musical color that is portrayed here in heaven as they all begin to unite in a beautiful call to worship. We see singers—some whom we recognize—whose music has thrilled us on earth, stand up to lead heavens choir. As they begin to sing, the entire assembly of millions upon millions of the redeemed join in the chorus. The throne room of heaven rings with worship and praise as our hearts rejoice. The anointing power and presence of God is so all-encompassing. We feel sensations that can only be described as the Father wrapping His loving arms tightly around us. It is as though we are embraced by our Father in the spirit. We feel such comfort and warmth in the presence of our loving heavenly Father. We praise God, the Creator of life and the Father of love. The love of an earthly father cannot be compared to the embrace of our heavenly Father. It is as though He has lifted each of us upon His knee and kissed our cheeks. Every fiber of our souls are alive! The entire stadium of heaven is filled with an electricity and fire of God's presence. He is truly enthroned in the praises of His people!

14

Covenant Deliverance
and Protection

From bondage to freedom, from slavery to sonship,
All through the water, covered safely by the blood.

Worship time in heaven's tabernacle, heaven's throne room, flows on for some time. No one wants to stop. However, the Father has much He would like us to learn. He was pleased with the display of love and worship from the family. We now hear His call for a pause in praise as He directs everyone's attention to our next speaker. *Story Time in Heaven* must resume.

One of the twenty-four mighty ones seated on a throne stands up. He has the appearance of a wise and strong leader. There is a brilliant glow about his face that brightly reflects the glory of God. He was a leader among men on earth, now an elder in heaven who was led mightily by God. Yet, he is a man who was meek above all the men on earth. His story is powerful, exciting, and will affect us all. This we seem to understand in the spirit. His transit on earth was very unique and impactful. As heaven's hologram opens and we enter in to the world of this character, he recounts that he was born about four hundred earth years after the time of Joseph, our previous speaker. He also was a descendant of Abraham, Isaac, and Jacob. The place of his birth was in Egypt. Things had changed greatly over those succeeding years. The pharaoh who loved Joseph had long since gone. With his departure, all that God had done through Joseph to save all of Egypt faded from memory. The children of Israel had grown large in number. God had blessed them as he had promised their ancestor Abraham. They had increased from approximately seventy people in Goshen to over two million people. Our speaker discloses that because they were so large in number now, the people of Egypt feared them. They feared that the Israelites as they were now called, might try to take over their nation or that they would join forces with an enemy. They feared that the Israelites would help their enemies conquer them. Rather than taking the risk that this might happen, the Egyptian leaders decided to make the Israelites their servants and slaves.

Visualized before us, we see God's people, the descendants of Abraham, working long hours by the sweat of their brow. We feel their weariness and pain as they are bowed down under the oppression and strain. The Israelites continued to grow in number so the Egyptians decide to kill all the male children at birth. It seems Joseph's dream has been turned into a nightmare! But then we remember God promised Abraham that his family would be going to Egypt and four hundred years later, his family would be leaving Egypt. God promised they were to possess the land where Abraham lived. This dignified elder standing before his throne reminds us that God's word is forever settled, made sure and established in heaven. What He says will come to pass!

A deliverer, a man of God, was being prepared. Our speaker reveals himself as Moses, a child favored and protected by God for a great purpose. Moses announces that the Father does not desire that he share the whole story of his life but he is to focus on a very significant part of his story that flows with the revelation of the covenant of blood. The Father is highlighting this important truth in our family story on this occasion. Therefore, he just familiarizes us with a few critical events. For the first few years of his life, his mother nursed him, taught him about the God of heaven and his family's history, and she loved him deeply. He was then taken into the pharaoh's household. Pharaoh's daughter had saved him from death as an infant when she found him in a basket along the Nile. His mother had hidden Moses for three months in her home after he was born to protect him from death at the Egyptian's hands. She then set him in a woven basket into the river, entrusting him to God for protection. His sister was watching over him from a distance. Pharaoh's daughter found him there when she heard him cry. She was touched with compassion and decided to adopt him as her son. Running up to Pharaoh's daughter, Moses sister asked her if she needed anyone to nurse the baby and so he was nursed and cared for by his own birth mother until the appointed time for Moses to be educated and brought into the palace of the king of Egypt. Moses conveyed that he spent forty years in the pharaoh's household, learning what it was like to oversee and lead an entire nation. He was considered a grandson of the pharaoh. He acquired all the worldly knowledge of Egypt and all the skills needed to rule a nation.

In his heart, his mother's words, his mother's love, and the Spirit of God continue to tug at his heart. One day, he saw an Egyptian mistreating and beating an Israelite. Moses was angered and killed the Egyptian. When word came to the pharaoh of what he had done, he had to flee for his life. The next forty years, Moses lived in the desert of Sinai, a fugitive from Egypt. There he worked as a shepherd and learned the hardships of desert life. He was humbled greatly. Many skills were acquired in the desert as well, which prove useful later. Those eighty years had prepared him for the most powerful, fruitful, and productive part of his life. God would use Moses in an amazing and powerful way. In the desert, Moses acknowledged that he had a supernatural encounter with God. He saw a bush burning yet it was not consumed. The strange site caused him to turn aside from his trail. He wanted to investigate this unique phenomenon. As he approached, the God of heaven spoke to him. He called him, empowered him, and commissioned him to be His representative. He was instructed by God to go back to Egypt. He was given directives to display God's power to the Israelites and the Egyptians and to lead the entire nation of Israel out of the land of Egypt.

In the giant hologram, we view the story quickly, one scene after another. There are conversations, confrontations, and miraculous displays of God's power over the gods of Egypt. Moses informs us that the main god worshipped by the Egyptians was the serpent, the one who deceived Eve and led Adam to sin, which brought on such catastrophe for all of mankind. The spirit informs us that when men see the glory of the heavens as it declares the majesty of our Father and they see the earth and the intricate handiwork of God but do not acknowledge and worship Him, men are led embrace lies and deception. These delusional deceptions are perpetrated by the serpent, the father of lies. The Egyptians did not follow the true way to fellowship with God instituted by the Father in the garden through the blood covenant. They did not follow Noah's example right after the flood by approaching God through the blood sacrifice, nor did they follow this plan expanded upon in covenant by Abraham and his descendants. This way of covenant sacrifice was God's idea, not man's. Although the practice of a blood covenant has been recorded on many continents and in many countries on earth, it became perverted by many of those who practiced the covenant sacrifice. The deviation from God's directions moved so far out from truth that they killed their own sons and daughters. Many perverted their worship to include not only human sacrifice, but lewd, sexual, sensual, and evil practices alongside them. In some areas of the world, this perversion even led to cannibalism. How far man falls when he worships the creatures of creation rather than the Creator!

Because the serpent was so esteemed in Egypt, God instructed Moses to throw down his staff in the pharaoh's presence, and it became a serpent. The deceiving false prophets, the sorcerers of Egypt, threw down their staffs as well and they also became serpents. What happened next shocked everyone present. Moses' serpent consumed the serpents of the Egyptians before it returned to a staff in Moses' hand. This first sign was to show the pharaoh who thought himself to be powerful like their serpent god that he was powerless to resist the word of God. God spoke in covenant with Abraham that his descendants would leave Egypt with great possessions at this very time, and no word of God can be stopped by mortal man. No man-made, man-imagined or man-worshipped god can resist or hold back the declarations of the powerful Word of the one true God, the Father of love. Moses reminds us that God watches over His Word to perform it. This sign was followed with many plagues on Egypt. They worshipped the River Nile that flowed through the land and nourished the plant life. It was filled with fish they consumed. So rather than worshipping the God who created rivers and fish, they worshipped the things He created. God turned the river to blood. This made it undrinkable and all fish within it died. We watch in the hologram as God also sends such deep darkness that it blots out the sun, another creation of God they worshipped rather than the Creator. He fills their homes with frogs, flies, and then lice, even in the palaces of the pharaoh. One plague after another, still they refuse to acknowledge God. The Lord then sent hail. Then it rained fire, destroying the crops. He sends locusts and caterpillars by the millions to eat the produce of their land. Again, Pharaoh refused to submit to the one true God of heaven and earth. Though they had boils on their bodies, their livestock and crops were being destroyed, and their land was being judged by Almighty God, still the pharaoh refused to yield to God's will and His word to let His people go.

Perhaps one day we will hear the story in more detail, but we pause as one last powerful act of God will take place in Egypt. Following this, the pharaoh would finally acquiesce to God's will and let His people go. One last plague will assail Egypt. The hologram quickly sped through the nine plagues upon Egypt. This final plague we are about to witness, will not only free millions of people from Egypt, it will reveal truths that point to a miracle that has saved the lives of untold millions since that time. Before this final plague took place, the Israelites made a request of all the Egyptians. They requested from the Egyptians that the Israelites would be given their jewelry and treasures. God gave them tremendous favor as the Egyptians loaded them down with treasures. They thus fulfilled another prophetic promise God made to Abraham as they together had entered into covenant four hundred years earlier. He said not only would they go to Egypt, become slaves, and then leave four hundred years later, but they would leave with great possessions.

Moses indicates that as the final plague is announced, special instructions were given to the Israelites. It was announced that every firstborn male of man or beast would be killed that night. However, the God of Abraham, Isaac, and Jacob (the Great I Am) provided a way of escape from this plague for His people. Instructions were given that each household was to slay a lamb, collect its blood in a basin, and then spread its blood on the doorposts and lintel of their homes with hyssop. They were then to roast the lamb and eat every bit of it. This was a covenant meal, a symbol of the sacrifice that would one day be made for all eternity. All were commanded to eat it fully clothed for departure, with a staff in their hand, and ready for the exodus—out of slavery and into freedom. Any person who was outside the house would not be protected from the death angel. The instructions must be followed exactly as directed by God. They were not to leave the house until morning. Everyone must stay inside to be protected by the blood.

We view that night in the hologram of heaven, the death angel is moving across the land of Egypt. The firstborn of man and beast are dying, and we hear a great cry of sorrow and loss penetrate the night air. Some are screaming, some moaning, and many are crying out in agony. Not a single family in Egypt was untouched by death that black night. Moses informs us that every Israelite heard the sorrowful cry of Egyptians. Judgment was falling on that entire nation. Yet in Goshen, where the Israelites lived, no one is moving about. All the Israelites are indoors, protected by the blood on the doorpost and lintel for God had said, "When I see the blood, I will pass over you." We wonder how the blood of an animal could protect all these people. For a moment, the hologram dims as we all set our gaze upon the golden covenant box with the golden angelic mercy seat forming its cover. We see the glistening scarlet liquid flowing over it and down its sides. For a moment, the Son of God seems to change form into a lamb, slain with its blood poured out. Now we know why as our hearts and minds are enlightened.

Moses continues the narrative. It is the next morning, Egypt was in sorrow. However, the nation of Israel was being birthed. Nearly three million people would leave bondage and become a free people. A small family who entered the land and was eventually enslaved was leaving as conquerors by the power of God and carrying the riches of Egypt with them as plunder and back wages for the many years of slavery. Moses acquaints us with the fact that not one person among them was sick or feeble. The power of the blood not only provided protection and freedom, it gave supernatural healing in their bodies. The sickness and diseases of Egypt were left in Egypt. What an amazing view we have as men, women, and children walk out of bondage. The joy on their faces is unmistakable! We hear singing and laughter.

As they left Egypt toward their promised land, God went with them. He appeared as a pillar of cloud by day and a pillar of fire by night. How comforting that must have been to Moses and all the people. The intense daytime heat of the desert was cooled by the cloud and the cool and darkness of the night were warmed and illuminated by the Almighty. He also sent angel's food like a seed that could be made into bread each morning and quail for meat each evening. Millions of people were provided for daily. In addition, He opened a gash in the rocks and the fountains below gushed out water, which flowed like a river in the desert. The Red Sea opened before them so they could walk through it on dry ground. When the Egyptians tried to pursue, the same sea that had parted to provide a way to safety for them swallowed the Egyptians. They were drowned along with their horses and chariots. A tragic outcome when men fight God rather than believe Him.

Moses, in reciting the adventure, reminds us that our God is greater than any circumstance or problem. He has already provided a solution before the problem arose. We, as followers of God, are not to look only to the natural world around us when crises arise. We have a loving heavenly Father who provides for His own. His is not limited by time and space. The Creator can make a way where no way appears in the natural realm. The shouts of amen resound in heaven. We rejoice with Moses in the throne room of God.

15

Covenant Blessing

What is real, casts a shadow, and the shadow mimics the real.
The substance is reflected in the shadow, but
it is the real we desire to reveal.

In our imagination, we watch the gigantic hologram of heaven displaying before us, an awesome sight! We observe God showing himself to Moses, Aaron, Nadab, Abihu, and seventy of the elders of Israel. They see the glory of the God of Israel. Below His feet is a pavement of sapphire stone and about Him the glory of heaven, pure and clean.

This newly birthed nation was led to the foot of the mountain of God where Moses was originally called to service by the Great I Am! The entire nation at the foot of the mountain heard the voice of God. They feel the earth shake and tremble at His appearance and they are afraid. Moses warned them that this trembling fear of the Lord they were experiencing in His awesome presence and display of power; and the resulting awe, and reverence for the Lord would act as a stimulus to keep them from sinning. There at the mountain of God, Moses was led high up into the mountain to the very presence of the Almighty. He spent forty days and forty nights communing with the Lord and receiving very detailed instructions concerning the laws that would govern this newly created nation. He was also given direction for the construction of a tabernacle or place of worship. At this tabernacle, God met with Moses and the people. The plans he received were very specific because this place was to be like a mirror, a type of foreshadowing of heavenly things!

Moses, speaking to all the assembly in heaven's grandstand, begins to detail the wonderful plan that the Lord God had for His people. He would guide them, provide for their needs, protect them from harm, and be their covenant partner. They were to follow His direction and obey His commands. He would lead them into the promised land flowing with milk and honey. The responsibility of the people was only to trust and obey.

The Lord showed Moses an exceptional plan to organize and direct the Israelites. In the center of their camp was to be placed a courtyard and a tabernacle. Outside the courtyard to the north, south, east, and west, the twelve tribes of Israel (three on each side) were to make their encampment during their travel. The Shekinah glory of the Lord would reside in the center of the camp within and above the tabernacle. God took up residence with His people. When God directed them to move, His presence, in the cloud by day or the pillar of fire by night, would arise. It would lift above the tabernacle and begin to move. The Israelites were then to break camp and follow in whatever direction the cloud or the fire led. When they were encamped, the courtyard around the tabernacle would separate the people from the presence of God. Though God was present, not all could approach Him.

Moses said there was only one way to God since the day Adam sinned. The wage of sin is death. Without the shedding of blood, there is *no* remission or forgiveness of sin. Therefore, the first object the worshipper would encounter as he approach God's presence was the brazen altar where animals were offered as a burnt sacrifices for the sins of the people. Beyond that was the laver filled with water for cleansing. Inside the tabernacle, there were two rooms: the holy place and, separated by a beautiful thick curtain, the holy of holies. In the holy place, there was a golden candlestick on one side and a table of bread on the other side. Just before the curtain was a table with incense burning, giving off a sweet aroma. Beyond the curtain in the holy of holies was a rectangular golden box called the ark of the covenant. Upon it was a golden lid with angels facing each other at either end. Their wings were spread over the ark. It is in this exact location that the Shekinah glory of the Lord would reside. Individuals could not approach the holy of holies or they would die. Only absolute purity could survive in the presence of Almighty God. However, Moses told us of the fact that one person alone—and only once a year, on the Day of Atonement—could enter the holy of holies. This individual was the high priest. He was to represent the people. This high priest was to take the blood of the covenant sacrifice and sprinkle it over the mercy seat, the covering of the golden ark of the covenant. This did not completely cleanse the nation from sin, but it did act as a covering for their sin for a year. God would overlook their sin and keep His part of the covenant on credit, looking toward a final sacrifice that would truly cleanse and remove all sin. Moses declared that here at the mountain of God, and in many instructions and promises of God to follow, the covenant first instituted in the garden with Adam was deepened even further. Very detailed laws were given by God to Moses. They covered every relationship of man with each other and with God. The overarching and most concise version of all they expounded upon was found on two tablets of stone. Upon these tablets, the Ten Commandments were written by the finger of God.

The Ten Commandments

Thou shalt have no other gods before me.
Thou shalt not worship any graven image.
Thou shalt not take God's name in vain.
Remember the Sabbath day to keep it holy.
Honor thy father and thy mother.
Thou shalt not kill.
Thou shalt not commit adultery.
Thou shalt not steal.
Thou shalt not bear false witness.
Thou shalt not covet.

These were given to Moses when he met with God on the mountain. They were placed into the ark of the covenant. Without perfect adherence to these commandments, no one could enter the presence of God and live. Once a year on the Day of Atonement, blood sprinkled over the mercy seat above the ark as a sacrifice alone allowed man to be in covenant with God.

As Moses related the journey across the wilderness, we see another common thread of scripture. Somehow within man, there is the tendency to doubt, to distrust, to become distracted from the promises of God. There is a tendency to look at life through natural eyes, not eyes of faith. God with His mighty Hand delivered this nation of slaves from Egypt, but Moses continues, He took them out that He might take them into the promised land. It was only a short distance from Egypt to this land flowing with milk and honey. The traverse could be done in days yet it took forty years! As they approached this land of promise, Moses chose twelve men, one from each tribe of Israel. They were to be scouts to help them prepare for their deployment into the land to conquer and inhabit this promised place. As they scouted the land, the spies were impressed with the fruitfulness of the land. There was so much produce and all that they would need to live, to survive, and to prosper. However, they also noticed tall, strong warriors inhabited the land. Ten of the spies gave in to fear. Two, Caleb and Joshua, embraced the opportunity to inhabit the land by faith. Ten looked at the natural challenges apart from faith and apart from the promise and direction of God. They saw the warriors of the land as greater than the God they served. They saw themselves as weak, small, fearful, and alone. God called this response an evil report.

Truth is not accurately stating what appears in the natural dimension. Truth is accurately stating what appears in the supernatural dimension.

The natural facts may appear true, but God's Word and His promise is greater and more accurate than any natural situation. They should have known that and embraced the promise of God. Because they gave this evil report, fear was created in the entire nation. Though Caleb and Joshua tried to reason with them according to faith, the people still chose fear. The entire generation perished, wandering in the wilderness for forty years.

As we view this sad day from the hologram of heaven, we remember what Abraham shared with us all earlier. He said that God never failed to follow through on a single promise He had made to Abraham in his entire life. These descendants of his somehow think that faith is a leap! All assembled in heaven, as we watch the story unfold, know the power of faith in God's Word. Every manner of miracle is represented from their various lives. Every promise of God is sure and more solid than anything on earth. The earth was made by God through His word and is sustained by his word.

Eyes of faith see into another world that the natural mind can't see.
Faith does not discount what others see. Faith
takes into account what others cannot see.

Moses goes on to share that when faith is mixed with the promise, miracles happen. When doubt discounts the promise and faith is crushed, catastrophes happen. Eventually, another generation arose that would embrace the promise and enter the land. As Moses pauses in the narrative, another speaker arises. Joshua stands near Moses, his mentor, and adds another layer to the truths we are hearing and seeing play out in people's lives. Joshua reminds us that not every one of the spies sent in to check out the promised land gave an evil report of unbelief. He and Caleb declared a positive report, a report of faith!! Lest we misunderstand this point, Joshua states, "The doubts of others may delay your dreams, but only *your* doubts can destroy your *dreams!*"

When the generation that left Egypt died in the desert over a forty-year period, Joshua and Caleb only grew stronger in faith, greater in wisdom, and more confident in their God-given dreams. Caleb dreamed of a special mountain and city that he wanted to conquer and possess with his family! Joshua states that he was trained as Moses' successor, the one who would lead the nation in to the promised land. "When the time came, we both received the complete fulfilment of our dreams. Joshua added, "As for me and my household, we would always serve the Lord!"

Prior to conquering the land, God made it very clear the extent and contents of the covenant itself. We enter the scene, hear the sounds, and feel the excitement as the entire nation of Israel is assembled, six tribes of Israel are instructed to stand on Mount Gerizim to bless and six tribes are to stand on Mount Ebal to curse. A nation at the crossroads, millions of people had a decisions to make, a decision that will determine their destiny. Then the curses were recited in detail that would come upon Israel if it disobeyed God and their covenant relationship. After each curse was recited, all the tribes on Mount Ebal shouted in solemn agreement, "Amen!" This takes a considerable length of time, and the judgments that would be exacted for disobedience are devastating! It would inflict havoc, misery, and affliction upon the people who disobeyed. It would be an utter fiasco. This moment is very heavy, solemn, and sacred with long-term import and repercussions.

Decisions determine direction, therefore decisions determine destiny!

Then the exact opposite was recited. A proclamation of all the blessing of God that would come upon them and overtake them if they were faithful to the covenant of God with Israel. These were agreed to by the six tribes on Mount Gerizim. They were to be blessed in every way: blessed in the city and blessed in the field; blessed in the fruit of their body, their ground, and their livestock; blessed in their baskets and in their storage areas; and blessed when they come in and blessed when they go out. Every enemy that went against them were to be defeated and to flee in seven directions. God said they were to be blessed in their storehouses and in everything they set their hand to. They were to be blessed in the land God was giving them and established as a holy people unto God. The Lord also declared He would open unto them His good treasure. He would send the rain in season and bless all the work of their hands. He stated that they would be lenders and not borrowers. God also would make them the head and not the tail, above only and not beneath. What amazing promises from God!

Moses further declared that God set a stirring challenge before them. Heaven and earth were called to record this extraordinary moment. Millions of people had their future on the line. Moses swore solemnly that God set before them a choice between life and death, blessing and cursing. He then showed His heart and desire for them by saying, "Choose life that both you and your descendants will live!" They are urged by Moses to love the Lord, obey His voice, and cleave unto Him. He concludes by saying, "He is your life. He is your length of days. Do this so that you can dwell in the land promised to your forefathers, Abraham, Isaac, and Jacob."

Choice is your greatest power. You control your destiny with its use. Choose wisely!

As the hologram closes, Moses is still standing and finishing his adventurous story. We are struck by something far greater in import than what we have just witnessed. Long life, blessing, and favor— the involvement of God in our day to day activities is amazing! We embrace it, we receive it. But even greater is what we are viewing of eternity in heaven during this imaginary journey. Moses declares that regardless of how much we are blessed on earth, heaven outweighs it all. Moses declares he would rather suffer the challenges of the people of God than to enjoy the pleasures of sin for a season. Moses rejoices as he esteems Christ's greater riches than the treasures in Egypt. That is why he forsook Egypt, not fearing the wrath of the pharaoh because he saw Him who is invisible! On earth, Moses had heaven in view. Earth's treasures are wonderful. Heaven's riches are matchless, eternal and beyond the power of our imagination to fully comprehend.

16

Legacy of Faith

A life lived well never ends. Its legacy lives on.

In heaven's grandstand, Moses ends his epic adventure.

We pause to contemplate, digest, and absorb the importance of this saga. So many truths to mull over, meditate upon, and embrace as we enjoy this fantastic adventure. We are here as outsiders yet we feel like more than just visitors on this incredible imaginary tour of heaven. We feel a kinship; in fact, we feel as though we are already citizens of this amazing celestial city. Our view begins to change as we are directed to move out of the massive stadium with the throne room suspended above the center. As we walk out, our perspective changes. We see that the crystal-clear glassy floor of this massive stadium, has many layers of absolute clear flooring beneath our feet. The crystal sea is filled with millions of citizens as are the heights of the stadium surrounding this unique sea. Moving out from the throne room of heaven, we notice that the city itself is somewhat like a cube. The streets are layered upon one another in multitudes of layers. In the very center of this massive cube is the stadium of heaven and the throne room where all gather to worship. From this location flows the glory of God Almighty, the light of the city. There is no need for streetlights, power lines, or phone lines. God Himself gives light and power in this sacred, celestial place! The original, invisible, ethereal WiFi of heaven is the communication system of the spirit. The connection is instant and constant with unblocked access to all!

There is never any interference in the flow of life and information shared between individuals in the supernal city called heaven.

Moving out from the city into the vastness of eternity itself, we begin to realize even more the magnitude of heaven. As we noted earlier, the city is ever expanding. New streets, new mansions, and new arrivals are in a constant stream of life flowing from earth to heaven! Within the walls of this vast, heavenly cube, beautiful, golden avenues lined with mansions are expanding in all directions as we watch. No one arrives without a place prepared lovingly and thoughtfully by the heavenly Father's design. A place is prepared specifically for each individual and as unique as the fingerprints of their hands back on earth. Each citizen is a unique creation of God and are individually loved by their heavenly Father. Outside the celestial city is the vast openness of eternity. It is God's unending domain. The universe that He created for man off in the distance is minute, tiny, and so small compared to eternity. Here, time does not exist. We are in a completely different dimension, one that is not subject to the constraints and limitations of earth or the universe. On this imaginary adventure, we now realize we were made for more than what we have been. On earth, we are like the dew that appears and is gone with the warmth of the morning sun. Here in eternity with our Creator, our heavenly Father, eternal life has been prepared for all who will believe. Though our bodies were designed for the earth, our spirits were designed for eternity.

Far away, we see the universe God created to bring us life. It has dimmed so much in our view, like a small drop in a vast sea of space that flows into the limitless reaches of eternity. As man is so minute in the realm of the universe, so the universe is minute in the realm of eternity. Also, across this vast space of eternity, we see what appears to be the glow of a fire. Between the celestial city and this distant glow is a gigantic white throne room next to the library and media center of eternity. However, to discover these areas, we will need to take more of these imaginary journeys. From the throne room, the call is heard even outside the city. We somehow hear it in our spirits. It is the call to worship and the call to return to heaven's grandstand and to the glorious throne room of heaven. Much more must be heard. This travel in eternity is so amazing! Though we can meander through the streets, if we so desire, we can be instantly translated from one place to another as well. No car, no airplane, and no vehicles are needed. They are totally obsolete. A choice made, faith released, and the instant transfer from one place to another is made. I wonder if that was what happened with a deacon named Philip. I imagine he may have had this experience in a small measure while on earth. Perhaps we will hear his life's journey one day during *Story Time in Heaven.*

We feel compelled, drawn to answer the call to the throne room of heaven. From our place in eternity, we fly like angels into the city, flashing smiles as we pass through the pearly gates and down golden avenues viewing fabulous mansions, beautiful gardens, and lush green parks heading straight to the center of the city. In the company of multitudes singing and rejoicing, we enter the fabulous stadium of heaven. How we have longed to return to the throne room where the Father of love awaits. We feel joy. We feel exhilaration. We feel great anticipation. All are entering His gates with thanksgiving and His courts with praise. When we arrive in our place of observation, imagination, it seems, is on overload. *Wow,* what wonders we have all beheld! Each time we enter this awesome place, new understanding comes to our hearts. In this moment, I see precious believers worshipping in the throne room, people I had known on earth. My eyes fill with tears of joy.

One who stands out so clearly is a man whose life impacted mine greatly. His name is John. I knew he would be here! I was absolutely sure of it long before he left earth's domain many years ago. We would talk for hours and we often walked and prayed together. We enjoyed singing hymns of the faith. He loved to sing hymns about heaven. One of his favorites was, "We Shall See the King." In many of our conversations, he would talk about his father. It is a story impacted by heaven. John was the son of a minister, an itinerant evangelist. He told me the story many, many times. I loved to hear about his father's conversion and his call to the ministry. His dad was well-off for his day. He had land, cattle, a wonderful wife, and many children. He played the fiddle at dances, and he was a talented, prosperous young man. One fateful day, a traveling minister came through their small community in Southeast Oklahoma. He held prayer meetings in a tiny building near his father's land. After hearing their prayers and hearing the story of Jesus, John's father embraced Christ as his Savior! His conversion was deep and transforming.

John's father, Cully Stevens, loved to read the Word and pray. He committed himself completely to God and loved and worshipped His savior. One momentous day while he was walking through the fields, he sought God in prayer, kneeling in the dirt from which we were all made. In that moment, God gave Cully a vision of heaven. He saw the place we are visiting in our imagination and—though I don't know what he saw—it changed him forever! The vision of heaven was so real that it seemed to Cully that he was looking through a window into the very throne room of heaven! John told me that God spoke to his father. The Lord said, "Don't you see how real this is? Wouldn't you be willing to preach my gospel?" The answer was instant! His father said, "Yes, Lord!" He also asked one thing of the Lord, "Please save my family." From that day, he set himself to declare the truth of God's Word. He preached in churches, set up tents in towns all around, and shared the realities of heaven and the truth of God's Word as an itinerate evangelist. As a result, Cully led many souls to Christ!

Cully was my wife's grandfather, making his son John her father. John was one of my best friends in this life. His life, his influence, his example, and the stories he told have impacted my life forever! As I see John rejoicing in heaven, my heart is so full! Though he cannot see us (we are only here in our imagination), we can see him. I have never had the privilege of meeting his father Cully, but I love him. It is amazing how God's love can unite believers in the faith just by hearing about their lives despite never knowing them on earth. One day, we will embrace in heaven! I did meet Cully's wife, and what a wonderful woman of God she was and is! She is here as well. I see all three—Cully, his wife, and his son John—rejoicing in the presence of God! In addition to these here in heaven's throne room, I see many of his family members, Cully's other children and grandchildren as well. However, something surprises me about them. They were much older than they look when I last saw them on earth, yet in this realm of the spirit, they appear so young and vibrant as they rejoice in the presence of God! While they do not have glorified earthly bodies as yet, there is a youthful vigor and strength in their looks. I observe absolutely no weakness, illness, or pain at all! This is the life of the spirit.

Walking thru this earthly journey,
Other's lives have touched mine.
Leaving imprints; and a pathway;
Footprints in the sand.

My view expands, searching the citizens of heaven and seeing many others I recognize. My father, my grandparents, and many saints I have shared time with on earth are now residents of this glorious celestial city! They entered this magnificent place in faith by the grace of God!

Musicians are playing as heaven's choir is singing and glorifying the King of all kings and the Father of love. As they worship together, time is nonexistent as this is eternity. I hear songs that I know and many I have never heard before. All of them glorify the Lord. I join in heartily as everyone starts singing two of my favorites, "Amazing Grace" and "How Great Thou Art." To sing these songs in this heavenly place with saints from all nations, all races of earth, and all ages of time is inexplicably delightful. Together we become one family to glorify the Father and His Son, our Lord. Some lead with new tunes I have never heard but shortly we all join in singing with millions of voices of every type: soprano, alto, baritone, and bass. Every instrument known to man and some I have never heard accompany the singers as heaven's orchestra fills the atmosphere with praise. On some songs, I hear voices familiar to me, ones I loved to hear on earth. Each voice in heaven still holds its unique sound they alone use in praise. What a wondrous place it is as we visit heaven in our imagination. During this time of worship and praise, which could go on forever, individual voices echo throughout heaven's stadium in praising and glorifying the Lord.

A unique voice, one I have never heard before, begins a solo. Other voices are stilled, longing to hear this beautiful sound of worship. We are informed in spirit that this voice belongs to one of the greatest songwriters in history. He accompanies his song with his own unique instrument, an ancient harp. Though I have never heard the beautiful tune he sings or the unique beauty of his voice, I have heard these words before. Pouring from his heart in anointed worship, David sings one of his best known songs!

> The Lord *is* my shepherd; I shall not want. He makes me to lie down in green pastures' He leads me beside the still waters. He restores my soul; He leads me in the paths of righteousness for His name's sake. Yea, though I walk through the valley of the shadow of death, I will fear no evil; for You *are* with me; Your rod and Your staff, they comfort me. You prepare a table before me in the presence of my enemies; You anoint my head with oil; My cup runs over. Surely goodness and mercy shall follow me All the days of my life; And I will dwell in the house of the Lord forever. (Ps. 23, NKJV)

17

Covenant Power

Many know the covenant promises; fewer actually believe.
Still fewer lean upon them in faith and, thereby, receive.

We will now encounter new adventures and learn more powerful truths. Many of them revolve around the blood covenant, the covenant of love. Our Father has a purpose and a plan in all that He directs. As each of our previous speakers have noted, only a small part of their story—and now David's story—will be spoken, viewed, and revisited. By their words and in images displayed before us, we learn so much. The dynamic way we seem enter in to the experiences themselves through the mesmerizing hologram of heaven astounds me! We seem to experience in real time what they experienced in their travels on earth.

David the psalmist lays down his harp as he finishes one of the most beloved and well-known songs of the ages. The Father asks him to continue the family story. Standing before the assembled saints and in the presence of Almighty God, David begins to give an account of several significant events in his life. As the first episode commences, we are transported into the scene. The hills around the ancient city of Bethlehem come into view. Sheep are grazing on the grass-covered hillside. We observe a pond of still water and a stream flowing nearby. A short distance away is a lush green forest. As we gaze on the scene, a soft, gentle melodic sound is heard. A harp and a voice, with exquisite expressions of worship and of love, permeates the air.

A young man, a shepherd with a voice calming to the sheep, sings in worship and adoration to the God of heaven. From his earliest years, David had great talent for the playing of the harp. The sound was soothing and flowed from a gift deep within. Though many sought fame, fortune, or wealth, David had a heart after God. David was a descendant of Judah, one of Abraham's sons. He knew in detail their family history. The covenant of God had been made known to him from an early age. David knew the entire story from the first day of Adam's sin down to his present day. The accounts of Noah, Abraham, Joseph, and Moses—he knew them all! Following Moses and the wilderness journey, the Israelites entered the promised land. The commander of the army was Joshua while Caleb was among their great leaders.

Four generations later, David was playing his harp on the hillside. Many days and nights were spent in this quiet and delightful area as David watched over his family's sheep. He knew the best areas for grazing and the calmest places for them to drink. While on the night watches, he had an unobstructed view of the heavens with no competing lights nearby. There was no earthly source of light to dim, obstruct, or hinder his view of the night sky. Millions of stars, constellations, and galaxies displayed their majestic beauty. David saw the glory of God and acknowledged the Creator's hand. While observing the heavens, his heart would overflow with praise. On display in the hologram of heaven, we hear him playing his harp and singing from his soul as he relaxes on the hillside.

> *Lord, our Lord, how majestic is Your name in all the earth! You have set your glory in the heavens. When I consider Your heavens, the work of Your fingers, the moon and the stars, which You have set in place. What is man (human beings) that You are mindful of him and You care for them?*

David understood the loving care and the thoughtful eye of God was upon him. As he cared for his father's sheep, David understood that God also cared for His sheep. He knew also:

As a father has compassion on his children, so the Lord has compassion on those who fear Him for He knows how we are formed. He remembers that we are dust. Bless the Lord, O my soul, and all that is within me, bless His holy name. Bless the Lord, O my soul, and forget not all His benefits.

David sang, worshipped, and gained insight and revelation. He knew well that there were benefits for those who were children of the covenant. There were benefits for those who were circumcised, who offered the sacrificial lamb for their sins, and who observed the Passover each year. These covenant blessings set David and his people apart from all other people on this earth. God promised to provide for them, to protect them from their enemies, and to bless them mightily in this promised land. The land was theirs as the promise of God to Abraham himself. As David watched over his sheep, he not only led and guided them, he also protected them from wild animals. On two different occasions, his flock was attacked. Once a lion pounced on one of the sheep and carried it off in his mouth. The other occasion was of a bear coming out of the woods and grabbing one of his sheep. David was highly skilled with a slingshot. He practiced all the time along the creeks. He became extremely accurate with his shots. Using his skill with the sling and his knife and his faith in God, David pursued the lion and the bear. He killed them both and rescued his sheep. Though not tall in stature, David was strong in spirit. He was full of faith and courage. David was both a worshipper and a warrior!

As David is speaking in the heavenly grandstand, we are watching the scenes. One fateful day as David was with the sheep, a visitor came to the town of Bethlehem, Samuel the prophet. He was a judge and the greatest spiritual leader in Israel at that time. Samuel is on a mission from God. We see him conversing with David's father, Jesse.

They ask him if he comes in peace. Samuel acknowledges that he does and he has come to sacrifice to the Lord. He instructs the people to consecrate themselves and come to sacrifice with him. The actual reason is the king of Israel, Saul, disobeyed the Lord. The Lord told Samuel that he no longer approved of Saul because of his disobedience. He is sent by God to anoint one of Jesse's sons to be the next king of Israel.

Samuel consecrated Jesse and his sons. When they arrived, Samuel saw Eliab. He thought that surely Eliab was the Lord's anointed. He was very tall, as was Saul, Israel's first king. The Lord rejected him and instructed Samuel not to consider his appearance or his height. The Lord said that He saw things differently than people. People look at outward appearances, but the Lord looks at the heart. One by one, all seven of Jesse's sons pass before Samuel, but the Lord did not choose any of them. Samuel asked Jesse, "Are these all the sons you have?" There was one more, David, who was on the hillside tending the sheep. Called by his father, he appeared before Samuel. David was glowing with the glory of God. He was healthy and handsome. His appearance was exceptional. Samuel was instructed by the Lord to anoint David as the next king of Israel. Anointing oil was poured upon him in the presence of his brothers. From that very day, the Spirit of God came powerfully upon David. Because he was the youngest of the brothers, when the armies of Israel were at war, the older brothers went to join the battle. David stayed home to tend to the family's flock.

The scene is now changing. We see a panoramic view of armies preparing for battle. We hear the noise of many soldiers marching, pitching tents, and clanging shields and swords as they are assembling. One of the nations around them, living on land that had been promised to their ancestor Abraham, is waging war against the Israelites. This Philistine army arrayed themselves on the side of a mountain. They pitched their tents and gathered their forces to prepare for battle. Across the valley on another mountainside, Saul and the Israelites assembled and camped. They laid out their battle lines as well. Between these two armies was a valley and a gentle stream flowing over rocks, stones, and pebbles. Rather than either side launching an attack, something strange and interesting was happening.

On the Philistine side of the valley, one of their champions would step out from their ranks. He was massive in size, several feet taller than any of the Israelites. He was covered in protective shields and armor, and his sword was gigantic! The reach of his long arms and sword would kill anyone else before they could get within striking distance in one-on-one combat. He was not only huge in size, he was a very skilled, battle-hardened warrior. This man's name was Goliath. He was coarse, gruff, and bold. Each morning and then each evening, Goliath would issue a challenge to the Israelites, shouting boldly and mocking the Israelites. He would challenge them to send someone to fight against him one-on-one. Whoever lost, that nation's army would serve the other. This continued for forty days. Goliath's challenge generated fear and terrified the Israelite army. No one wanted to take on Goliath alone. He was legend in the Philistine army.

David changes the scene again as he begins to relate how his father Jesse, now a very old man, sent his three oldest sons into the battle with Saul but kept David at home home to tend to the sheep. Often, David traveled back and forth between their home and the battlefield. One day, Jesse sent David with bread and cheese for his brothers and some provisions for the commanders. He was sent to assess how the battle was going and to come back and assure his father that his brothers were okay. David left early in the morning and arrived at the camp when the soldiers were setting their battle lines. There were shouts on both sides of the valley as they all prepared for war. David saw what was happening. After leaving his supplies, with the one in charge of stores, he ran to the battle lines. David asked his brothers how they were doing. As they were talking, Goliath stepped out from the battle lines on the other side of the mountain and shouted his usual defiant challenge. David saw the Israelite army flee in fear and terror when Goliath challenged them. He also heard some of them discussing the disrespect Goliath showed to Israel. Continuing to listen. David also heard some of the soldiers recount a promise from King Saul that great wealth will be given the man; who would kill Goliath. He will give him his daughter as wife and exempt his family from taxes. David asked for clarification. "What will be done for the one who kills Goliath? Who is this uncircumcised Philistine anyway that he thinks he can defy the armies of the living God?" As he was speaking with the soldiers, his brothers became jealous and mocked him. They thought he was just conceited. David was brought before Saul. The king doubted that he could defeat Goliath because David was just a young man and Goliath has been a warrior from his youth. David told Saul of the lion and the bear that he killed when they attacked his flock of sheep. He assured Saul that the uncircumcised Philistine will end up just like the lion and the bear. The Lord who rescued David from the paw of the lion and the paw of the bear would rescue him from Goliath as well! Saul relented and let David go into battle.

We now see the gigantic, battle-hardened Goliath moving toward David as he stepped out from the Israelite camp to meet him. The brutal, foul-mouthed warrior Goliath was experienced in battle. He was filled with disdain, despising this handsome young man half his size that the Israelites sent out to meet him. Goliath was fully armed for battle, confident in his ability and skill. He knew he would make quick work of this foolish young man. Goliath called to David, "Come here," he said. "I will give your flesh to the birds and the wild animals!"

David had taken no armor though Saul offered his own. When he was trying it on, it just did not fit. David knew one very important principle. *You cannot walk in someone else's faith and achieve victory. Battles in life are personal to an individual. You win or lose, succeed or fail, by your own faith.* He walked in the faith of God. He had his shepherd's rod and his sling. David stopped by the creek down in the valley to get five smooth stones. He heard Goliath had four brothers. With the stones in his shepherd's bag, the staff in one hand, and the sling in the other, David approached the Philistine. Then everything changed. David said boldly to the Philistine, "You come against me with a javelin, a sword, and a spear, but I come against you in the name of the Lord God Almighty. He is the God of the armies of Israel. He is the one you have defied! Today, the Lord will give you into my hand. I will strike you down, cut off your head, and give the carcasses of the Philistine army to the birds and wild animals. The whole world will know that there is a God in Israel! Everyone here will know that it is not by sword or spear that the Lord saves. The battle is the Lord's."

How the tables have turned! Normally. It seemed impossible for David to win. But David charges at Goliath; takes a stone from his sling; and, anointed with great skill by the Lord, and directed by the Spirit of God, he let the stone fly. Like a bullet, it struck Goliath directly in the forehead. He fell facedown on the ground. David used Goliath's own sword to cut off his head.

How could this happen? What was the reason? David informs everyone assembled in heaven's grandstand that because he was a child of the covenant, God fought his battle for him and won the day. Circumcision was one of the signs of the covenant. David was circumcised; Goliath wasn't. This was the difference between life and death. It has always been so. Many know of the covenant, David informs us, but fewer believe in its power. Of those who believe, even fewer receive, unwilling to put faith to the test. Without faith, it is impossible to please God. Every Israelite in the army of Saul was a member of the covenant family of God! "That day;" David declares, "only he actually believed in its power." Any of the Israelites were more than a match for Goliath if they would believe and act on God's promise that when Israel's enemies attacked, they would flee before them seven different ways.

Here in the portals of glory, we have been viewing an awe-inspiring adventure. As we meditate on what we have witnessed, we see is a simple picture. It is a pattern, an example that declares one of the most important of eternal truths. A covenant relationship based on the blood, when believed and acted upon, brings victory and reward! Out of an entire nation in our previous story of Joshua and Caleb, two men believed in the covenant and the promise. However, an entire generation of Israelites around them perished *because they believed what their natural eyes saw more than the covenant with God.* The promise of God was not mixed with faith in their hearts. The good news in that preceding account is that Caleb and Joshua believed and possessed the land of promise. So in this epic battle just enacted, a nation of soldiers in covenant ran away from the battle, trembling in fear. Why? Because though they had a promise, it was not mixed with faith. There was one, unique covenant man among them named David. He mixed the promise with faith then faced the enemy and won. He won not only for himself, but for the entire army of Israel!

In our imaginary place here in the throne room, we wonder how different would life be on earth if in our hearts, we saw life from this perspective of heaven? What a thought—*living in the light of eternity*!

18

Covenant Love

In covenants of love, in covenants of blood,
Two parts become one as two destinies unite.

David continues to guide our thoughts with his words. He informs everyone in heaven's throne room that years later, he would become king of Israel. He had already been anointed for the task by the prophet Samuel. The heavenly Father interjects "It was not David's outward appearance, but his heart that qualified him for leadership." We know it has been said by many that David was a man after God's own heart, not perfect in all his actions but quick to repent. He was a worshipper, a warrior, and a believer. Taking up the discourse again, David informs us that covenant principles were the foundation from the beginning in worship of our Father God. Blood covenant principles were well-known on the earth within many nations on every continent. The Lord Himself initiated covenant worship on the first day of man's sin in the garden of Eden. In fact, He already instituted the covenant in his heart from the foundation of the world. God the Father slew a lamb. He shed its blood, and poured it out on the earth to cover Adam's sin. This lamb's skin was then used to cover man's nakedness. This action was a necessary part of worship, required with regularity according to the direction of God. King David continues to give us certain facts as the hologram begins to open and visualize his story. Every Israelite father, from the king's house to the servant's quarters, were urged by their Father God to instruct their sons regarding these covenant truths.

As we enter the scene opening before us, we see a magnificent palace of many fine rooms. It is an impressive structure constructed on a hillside using large rectangular limestones, massive in size and very heavy. These materials had been shaped and transported to the site from quarries. Many of the famous cedars of Lebanon are used in this beautiful edifice. The stone-and-wood structure of Phoenician design used native rock as a base and cut limestone building blocks as a long stairway up from the valley below. Long open porticos with ceilings twenty feet high supported by twin columns of limestone every few feet greet those who ascend the stairway. The limestone stairway and porticos are bordered and adorned with carved limestone figures. Along the stairway on either side are massive carved lions, the symbol of the tribe of Judah. Carved in the columns are depictions of stories relating to David's history and that of the twelve tribes of Israel. They highlight important people or moments in their history. These adorned colonnades supporting the portico outside the palace tell stories to all who examine and ponder their meaning.

We notice two large rooms, one is a throne room and the other a large area for entertaining. They have high ceilings and double-column supports. Throughout the palace area, we find many rooms. These interior walled sections are constructed out of cedars from Lebanon. The ceilings in these cedar rooms are lower and also made of cedar. Many such sections are found throughout the palace. Some are designed for public ceremony and royal business. Several of the larger rooms had cedar ceilings while others, such as the throne room, are twenty feet high with a ceiling of limestone. Other areas are set aside for David personally and for his very large family. The columns and pillars supporting the interior ceilings and walls and many of the furnishings in this section are cedar. Because the palace was across a valley from the city of Jerusalem, the view from the city was incredible!

We ascend the stairs past porticos, impressed with the reverse view of the city of Jerusalem from this side of the valley. We enter the royal palace of David, the king of Israel. Guided past the throne room and the royal reception hall, we are escorted directly to a place where few are allowed, the private family quarters of the king. We gain access to a delightful area of peace, pleasure, and relaxation. Comfortable bedchambers with private sitting areas line a hallway as we are guided into a plush gathering place enjoyed by the family of the king alone. Smiling, we are inserted into the scene unseen by anyone there.

We listen as David is conversing with a group of young men of varying ages. These young men, we learn, are David's sons. They are in their father's presence for instruction and fellowship. As other men of his day; the king feels responsible in participating in the education of his sons. On occasion, he would meet with them individually to answer questions and guide their learning. On this beautiful day, the chamber they are in has a raised seat for their father. The young men are sitting or reclining on comfortable oversized cushions on the polished stone floor. One exterior wall has a large opening with a grand, awe-inspiring view. We gaze through the beautiful portico, across the valley toward the city of Jerusalem. Framed by this opening is a prominent view of one section of the city directly before them. David's attention is continually drawn to this area. It is where David desires to build a temple for the Lord, his God. We listen in on this imaginary voyage as though we are genuinely there. The multidimensional hologram of heaven seems to place us within the scene. How it enlivens and enhances the experience more than we could ever have imagined were possible!

David has been talking to his sons about a very special friendship that began just after he defeated Goliath. He often shares with his sons the importance of the blood covenant relationship that they had with Yahweh, the Great I Am, their Lord. He shares the story as it had been passed on down through history to their time today. His sons know about Noah, Abraham, Joseph, Moses, and a vast number more of their ancestors who walked in covenant with God. They *know* why they were circumcised and why they offer sacrifices. David shares these stories often with his sons. Today though, David has been thinking about another kind of covenant. It is not a covenant with God, but a covenant with another man. We are taken in David's storytelling with his sons to the point when he defeated Goliath. His sons love this story! It has always made them proud to hear of their father's victories, which were many. Goliath's defeat is what started it all and his eventual climb toward the throne after God anointed him to be king by Samuel. Rather than talking about Goliath today, David tells his sons of a very special friendship with King Saul's son and heir to the throne, Jonathan.

Right after the battle and defeat of the Philistine army, David and Jonathan met. They both recognized something special in each other. These young men had a deep faith in God. Courageous hearts burned within them. The covenant of blood with God was reverenced and respected. From the moment they met, they were drawn to a deep friendship, trust, and respect for each other. David told his sons that he and Jonathan entered a covenant relationship of love, a very sacred bond that not only David and Jonathan had, but all their descendants were in covenant together as well! Each one pledged in their covenant that all they had and all they possessed was at the disposal of their covenant partner and friend. As was the custom with such covenants, they exchanged garments. David said Jonathan gave him his robe, his symbol of status as King Saul's son and heir to the throne. Jonathan also handed him his belt that held his armor in place, signifying he would protect David. He even handed his covenant friend his sword and bow. Jonathan also promised to fight for David. David did the same for Jonathan. They pledged to protect and fight for each other and provide for their covenant partner's families through all generations. As a part of the covenant, often participants would cut into the palms of their hands until they bled and then they grasped hands. As their blood mingled, it symbolized the mingling of their lives and futures. David and Jonathan looked each other in the eye and declared the promises of support and aid to each other and to their descendants. They declared curses upon each other if they failed to live up to the promises made so solemnly that day. Truly, their word was their bond. They were, now and forever, blood brothers, covenant partners, and the dearest of friends. This practice may have been the origin of the handshake.

King David reminisced about some of the great battles they fought together. He also told his sons about Jonathan's bravery even before David ever met Goliath. Jonathan attacked a Philistine garrison, just him and his armor bearer. He asked the Lord for direction and favor and obeying the promptings of God's spirit, he led the army to a great victory. Jonathan was known throughout all Israel for his bravery, loyalty, and love. They became such great friends! David tells his sons, "We truly loved each other as we loved our own souls."

With his sons around him, David told them of how Jonathan interceded before his father, King Saul, to protect David's life. Jonathan did this on various occasions. Because Saul lost the kingly anointing through disobedience, he became fearful, hateful, and mean. An evil spirit would often oppress him, causing him great distress. Much of Saul's misery had to do with his unreasonable fear of David. Because David was anointed by God and had a heart after God, he was blessed mightily. When the armies would return from battle the women would sing, "Saul has killed his thousands, and David has killed tens of thousands!" This infuriated Saul and created anxiety, fear, and hatred in his heart toward David. But, David shares with his sons that Saul had nothing to fear from him. Saul had been anointed king and he would never do anything to harm God's anointed one. David was a worshipper and the presence of God and the anointing was upon him and his music. He was often summoned to play music for King Saul. This would soothe his troubled spirit. Many times, Saul continued to be overcome with anger and hatred. He would then attempt to kill David with a javelin. Thankfully, the Lord would protect David, and Saul's javelin would miss its mark. Over time, Saul's hatred for David increased. Even though David was his son-in-law, being married to his daughter Michal, Saul devised plans to kill David. Michal and her brother Jonathan were aware of the king's hatred and evil plots to destroy David. Michal loved David. She warned him to flee their home one evening, helping him escape through a window after she heard of her father's plans to kill David the next morning. He posted guards at their doorway. She delayed the troops by placing a decoy on his bed. Michal notified the soldiers that David was ill. By the time they knew the truth,

David had escaped from the city. Later, Jonathan warned David to stay away from a weeklong celebration and banquet that was prepared. This was a special yearly ceremony taking place in the palace. Though he had a designated place at the kings' table, Jonathan urged David to stay away for a few days. He wanted to make certain it was safe for David to return to the palace. However, Saul harshly attacked Jonathan when David did not appear. In return, Jonathan urged David to flee. His life would be in peril should he ever return.

For many years, David recounted to his sons that he was an outcast in Israel. The king sent armies to destroy him. But God protected him and he had a special friend, a covenant friend. The king's own son was his covenant partner. Most important of all, David said, "I had the protection of the Lord our God. He preserved my life on so many different occasions throughout this time of exile." David proclaims to his sons, "What would have become of me had I not believed that I would see the Lord's goodness in the land of the living?" David opens his arms in gestures that say "Look around you at all we have today!" As they all gaze around the palace and out the window to the beauty of the city across the valley. "Remember, my sons," David says, "the Lord is faithful. He is our strength, our fortress, and our high tower of defense! One of the saddest days of my life, was the day I heard that the enemies of Israel killed both Saul and his son Jonathan. My heart broke! Even though Saul had gone back on God and hounded me mercilessly, he was originally anointed by God to be Israel's first king. He was Michal's father and my best friend's father. How my heart was grieved that dreadful day. I was even more saddened because of the loss of my covenant partner and friend, Jonathan. I wept much for this very great loss! Never has a man had a better friend."

His sons know these events happened many years ago. King David informs them that he had a very special reason for reciting this unique story today. He thought of Jonathan so often over the years but the constant battle with enemies as he was establishing the kingdom of Israel took up so much of his focus. Now that he had rest for a time from war during last few days and weeks, he thought more often about Jonathan. He remembered the covenant of love that they embraced so solemnly. Though he heard that all of Saul and Jonathan's family were dead, he ordered an inquiry to see if any of them were still alive. David reminded his sons that the promise of the covenant with Jonathan was to flow to their children, as well. He desired deeply to find a way to bestow kindness to any of his posterity on Jonathan's behalf. After a diligent search was made, David was informed that Jonathan had a son named Mephibosheth. He was five years of age when Jonathan was killed in battle. Those who cared for him in Saul's household feared that he would be killed as well. Mephibosheth would be an heir to Saul's throne! His nurse fled Jonathan's home with the child. In her haste, she dropped Mephibosheth, which badly damaged his feet. From that day on, though hidden and safe, Mephibosheth became lame. With his feet irreparably harmed, he was unable to bear his weight. Mephibosheth had been living in Lo-debar. He instructed his sons that another place will be set at the dinner table every night from that day forward for Mephibosheth. He informed his sons that he has commanded Mephibosheth to be brought to the palace. He will receive him at dinner today. "Each of you will greet and welcome him as one of the family. He shall eat at our table for the rest of his life. This is my covenant of love responsibility. It is also my great honor to have the son of my best friend here, alive and dining with us tonight."

As he finishes the story, it is now dinner time in the palace. The sun is setting behind the hills outside as David's sons make their way to the royal dining room. All the invited guests are arriving. David is the last to enter. Everyone rises as he makes his way to the long polished cedar table. The entire room is lit with beautiful candles. Many golden candlesticks line the hall on either side. We see the incredible craftsmanship of the tables, chairs, walls, and ceiling made by the craftsmen of his friend, King Hiram. Every room in this palace has a rustic appeal, yet there is warmth, beauty, and an elegance about the entire structure. This dining room has a polished stone floor with beautiful cedar beams, braces, walls, and ceiling overhead. The aroma of the wood and candles mingling with the divine smell wafting from the outside kitchen is mouthwatering!

On the table itself are many decorative plates, each setting uniquely made by craftsmen skilled in bronze. In the center at various points along its length, the table is illuminated by candlesticks of gold alongside large platters of gold and silver, which hold fruits and vegetables from all over his kingdom. Some exotic fruits were brought in by his friend Hiram's ships from all over the world. Around the walls are beautiful plaques made of ivory and ebony. The detailed workmanship is undoubtedly the finest in the world for his day. The surrounding walls and beams themselves have carvings of various designs depicting the life of David. Above and outside the wooden enclosure of the dining area; viewed as we see through the wide openings of the doors, massive columns of stone rise to a height of at least twenty feet. They support the higher structure above on this high point surrounded by valleys. The palace can be seen from the city, from a great distance across the valleys, and from the opposite sides of the Kidron Valley below. The glow of the setting sun upon the stone walls soon gives way to the reflective glow of bright lights burning on large stakes placed along the carved stone stairway, the colonnade, and portico.

King David looks up and down the table, nodding his head and greeting his guests. When David takes his place at the head of the table, everyone notices something unusual. There is one extra setting at the table tonight near the king in the section where his sons are seated. Everyone is puzzled by the missing guest. Many of the kingdom's leaders are here for this special meal. They were personally invited by the king. He has an announcement to make, they were told. Many of his mighty men are there on this night, men who have fought beside David and served their king well. These are all individuals who are leaders in his army or significant members of his government. Who was missing? Who would refuse the king's invitation? People wondered as King David takes his seat. Before dinner is served at the appointed time, David has requested the last invited guest to makes his arrival. He is escorted into the presence of the king with the assistance of Ziba who had been King Saul's servant. Mephibosheth bows prostrate before King David and says, "Behold your servant!" He was afraid, not knowing at that moment why he was summoned to the king's dinner. David reassures Mephibosheth that he has nothing to fear from the king. David informs him that because of the covenant he had with his father Jonathan, he will show kindness and bless him. Mephibosheth will be given all the land of his grandfather Saul and will eat at David's table always. David calls Ziba forward and makes a royal proclamation in the presence of all at the dinner that night. All of Saul's land will be given to Mephibosheth. Ziba and his sons will work the land and bring in all the produce for their master Saul's grandson so that he will have a means of support. However, Mephibosheth shall eat at David's table as one of the king's sons. David's sons welcome him to the table as he is seated near their father. All the guests, leaders, and great men greet Mephibosheth and welcome him to this new place of prominence. As platters of luscious food are being served, Mephibosheth sits at the table of the king.

We observe this dining room through the hologram of heaven. We ponder the power of the covenant of love. The blood covenant is established by two individuals on earth, but its benefits reach to succeeding generations. Then to our delight, we consider how much more powerful we should deem a covenant between God the Father and His Son, our Lord. A covenant done in our behalf and whose benefits reach to all in the family of God. Truly, this is a better covenant with even greater benefits. One day in our glorified bodies, we too will eat at the king's table, but that is for another imaginary journey to heaven.

19

Preparing a Place

David is a psalmist, a singer, a musician, and a worshipper. He loves to dance before the Lord. As the scene around David's dining room fades and the hologram of heaven dissolves before us, David remains standing in the assembly of heaven. He is smiling and rejoicing at the memory of this wonderful day. Having finished his narrative, David begins to sing about the covenant of love. This is an original tune with new words inspired by the spirit that have never been sung before. The song flows from David's heart under the spirit's anointing. The words glorify the Father's love and rejoices in the covenant that allows everyone present to be in this glorious place. We are in the presence of the King of all kings and the Lord of all lords. As David dances and sings, heaven's throng from all ages past unite with him in praise. Heaven's choir sings along. We now hear the orchestra of heaven with vibrant enthusiasm as great crescendos ring out. Heaven's grandstand of saints harmonize together with exuberant delight!!

For the first time, we become cognizant of two new activities or phenomena that escaped our view during previous occasions of praise in God's throne room. First, we become aware that white-robed dancers are rejoicing before the presence of the Lord. With grace, beauty, and artistry, these dancers express in movement what others express in voice and instrumental skill. The dancer's movements in colorful gestures display smooth and artful expressions of worship, glorifying God with the dexterity of their form and adding to the magnificent pageantry of these spectacles of worship. The expertise of these gifts, designed and given by God and so artfully displayed, undoubtedly are being exercised for the very purpose of their creation. Profuse praise proclaims His glory and grace! The second phenomenon we experience is the unique action of the rainbow above our father's throne and the matchless and beautiful way it reacts in the midst of praise. The rainbow is a magnificent, multifaceted arch of color that glistens and pulsates, keeping time with the harmonious vibration of the musical worship rising from heaven's citizens! The colors seem to transform in appearance and hue with the tone and the rhythm of the sounds. The rainbow reflects and enhances our view of the throne of the Father and of the Son. Gold, ivory, scarlet, blue, indigo, violet, emerald, and untold other shades of luminous color cast their glow upon the throne of God. It gives the effect of living light itself as it flows in glowing beauty within the Shekinah glory that surrounds our Sovereign's throne. What awe-inspiring depth and beauty this living light gives to all we envision. The gigantic grandstand of heaven filled with a multitude of saints in white robes singing, playing, or dancing adds to the sublime beauty of this amazing scene. To our eyes, their garments appear to glow! Their extraordinary robes emit a radiant reflection of the brilliant rainbow of colors shining in the Shekinah glory cloud around the Lord. Breathtaking, impressive, and sublime! Words fail in the description of this majestic view of worship around God's throne.

Eventually, the tempo of the music slows down as they move into a worshipful, melodious refrain, declaring the beauty of God's amazing grace. David takes a seat on his throne. He is one of the twenty-four elders facing the central thrones of the Father of love and His Son. All eyes, all hearts, and all minds, basking in the glory of God's presence, are focused upon the Father of love. All are drinking in deeply of the life and breath of God. I personally sense deep within words so familiar, words I have spoken in prayer daily back on earth. "Our Father, which art in heaven, hallowed, hallowed, hallowed be thy name!" These words were inspired and taught by the Son of God Himself! Never have these words seemed so real as they do in this moment.

There is much more to be told. As a prelude to this upcoming section of the narrative, we are taken back for a brief look at the beginning of the story. The Father of Love motions to the entire family of God rejoicing here to pause in their expressions of worship. The Father continues *Story Time in Heaven*. The Lord of Heaven and earth makes known His purpose in this assembly. Our gathering in this place is to specifically highlight the power of *dreams*, the repercussions of our *choices*, and the value and power of the *covenant of love*. The Father reminds us of the purpose and the design in His heart when He created a magnificent universe and then birthed within it a son. The Creator's desire, His heart, and His passion was to create a family that of their own free will would recognize, honor, and follow His directions. The heavenly Father longed to replicate Himself within His children. He desired that they would learn about their Father and that they would live together forever as a family. Our loving heavenly Father states that though our bodies were created for this earth, He designed man's spirit for eternity. He has plans for our bodies in eternity as well. They will be transformed in an amazing way and will be reunited with our spirits. God also makes it very clear that He loves and has loved everyone who has ever been born into this family from the beginning of time. His greatest delight is— and always has been since that first day in the garden—to bless and have fellowship with His children. However, many have not cooperated with His plan. Many chose to go their own way and reject His instructions, guidelines, and directions. Mankind, in general, had little understanding about the intricate ways that all things are designed to work in harmony. Everything is synchronized so that nothing is independent of effect on the other and indeed the universe around them. When there is rebellion to the Father's directives, great harm can be done to the balance of all that the He has created. Our Father reminds the assembly of saints that *man is not an independent, self-created master of his own destiny. Apart from God, he would not exist.* Apart from fellowship with the Creator, the Heavenly Father, man's spirit is dead. Man's very breath, design, heartbeat, and physical life depends upon the sustaining Word of God. *To selfishly declare that a lump of clay, a piece of dust, has no responsibility to respond in obedience to its Creator is absolute foolishness!*

When men see the magnificence of God's creation but do not glorify Him in their response and are not thankful to the Father God for their very life, they become dark, foolish and evil in their imagination and actions. Pride, conceit, and smugness leads men to think they can become their own masters. Yet this unlawful and rebellious action itself binds them to another master—a very dark master. As a result of this decision, many men have given their allegiance to an alien invader rather than to their heavenly Father. One of the serious consequences of this rebellion is that not only their life on earth is dramatically altered, but their eternal destiny as well. Rather than eternity spent with the Father of love and His family, it will be spent in a place designed for the alien invader, the father of lies. It is his cause that they have embraced. Our Father makes this point clearly to us. He declares, "Choices matter." Though men may have the ability to choose evil, it has consequences. Our Father reminds us that there is a vast difference between ability and authority. Just because man has the ability to do evil, it does not mean he has the *authority* to do evil. Adam had the ability to eat of every tree in the garden of Eden, but he did not have the authority to eat from every tree.

Sin separates, disobedience defiles, and rebellion is repulsive.

Hearing this, everyone in heaven's stadium quietly ponders the effects of the *power to choose*. Each one thankful in their own hearts that they chose wisely to serve and follow the Lord while on earth.

As we reenter the adventures of *Story time in Heaven*, the Father shares that following David's leadership in Israel, his son Solomon came to the throne. At the beginning of his life, his heart was so wise. David had instructed his son well. "When I asked Solomon what I could give him as a gift in leading my people," the Father says, "he requested neither gold nor fame or even long life. He requested an understanding heart to lead wisely. The request pleased me, therefore I gave Solomon an understanding and wise heart. There has never been any man as wise as Solomon before or after him. I also gave him riches, honor, and a long life."

We are also informed by Solomon as he rises to address heaven's multitude that the God of his forefathers chose him to build a temple. It was to be constructed in the area where Abraham was willing to sacrifice his son. This magnificent temple was designed after the pattern of the tabernacle that was presented to Moses. Both the tabernacle in the wilderness and the temple of Jerusalem were fashioned after things here in heaven.

The hologram of heaven appears before us and an entrance opens up. We are captured by its magnetic pull as we are admitted into the scene of Jerusalem around 960 BC. As we enter the living story, we are viewing a much larger Jerusalem than in David's time. Construction is taking place all over the city, a prosperous and growing city. A panoramic view shows two main areas of growth. One section of the city contains an impressive royal palace that dwarfs the one David built. However, there are similarities in style because some of the same builders are involved. It is the Phoenician king Hiram who has sent laborers and supplies to Solomon as he did for his father David. Solomon's palace area is massive but only partially completed. The second main area of construction is the temple area itself.

We observe great crowds in the city today. They all look extremely excited about an upcoming event that is to take place the next day. The city is so packed that many have pitched tents all around the city just for a place to sleep. Every shop owner is busy with customers. Food vendors are set up in the marketplace. Sidewalk vendors are displaying their wares along the narrow streets. All appear to be busy, selling their amazing variety of products. Bustling crowds jostle their way among the visitors on cobblestone ways. Homes are packed with friends and family from all over Israel—in fact, from around the world. Something momentous is obviously about to happen in Jerusalem. We now see the beauty of Solomon's palace. It is spectacular! The palace compound contains several sections for his many family members. Solomon has a vast number of exotic wives and a large family to house. One very unique section of Egyptian style and design has been constructed with great care for a pharaoh's daughter. Many articles of clothing and furnishings from her homeland in Egypt were acquired and transported to Jerusalem for her comfort. This was planned for and provided when she and Solomon were married. Her quarters are similar in size to the accommodations of the king himself. Each has a covered porch and an enclosed garden for private relaxation. One area of the palace of impressive size is the haram, shared by his numerous wives from nearby nations who have come to him with their unique traits, habits, and gods.

We also notice an impressive banquet hall just off the main courtyard. The long cedar dining table fills the length of the entire room. Along the walls and on the beams are beautiful carvings of great artistry and beauty. Exquisitely carved wooden candlesticks overlaid with gold leaf stand along all four walls. Smaller versions of these gorgeous golden candlesticks are placed upon the table as well. All the goblets on the table are pure gold. Baskets of fruit from many lands, breads of various types, and unique flavors of cheese. This bounty speaks of the reach of Solomon's influence and the blessing of Jehovah. Tonight a large group of dignitaries from around the world will gather for dinner. It will be only the finest cuisine in the world prepared masterfully for his guests this day. Vegetables, meats, fish, and fowl—Solomon always had the very best.

The outer skeleton of the main structures consists of very large hewn stones. The city wall surrounding Jerusalem was constructed of these massive quarried and precut stones as well. Within the large outer limestone skeletons of these impressive edifices are erected a framework of buildings made of cedar from Lebanon. Everything is fashioned of cedar and hewn stone. Large cedar beams support the interior ceilings throughout the palace. Within the buildings are magnificent treasures from all around the world. We behold silver plates, gold goblets, and glistening jewels in great abundance. Solomon loves beauty so we see many different varieties of plants, flowers, and trees in garden areas throughout palace compound. In one section of the palace grounds are stables for horses with archways for chariots and a well-supplied armory. In this area we observe the living quarters for the royal palace guards. Further on, we find the servants' quarters for the many who serve the king and his family. Only about half of the area enclosed within the outside walls of

Solomon's palace is completed at this time as construction continues daily with much more to be added over the years ahead.

The most notable and consequential portion of the palace is the court of judgment. At the top of a long stairway overlooking a massive courtyard sits an exquisitely carved throne covered in ivory and overlaid with pure gold. This majestic gilded ivory throne glows in the refection of the sun between massive limestone columns in a covered colonnade. A footstool of gold is at the base of the throne, and the armrests are overlaid with gold. Large limestone lions, the symbols of the tribe of Judah, Solomon's ancestors, stand guard on either side of the throne. Twelve lions in total sit on either side of the six-step platform plus there are two massive lions beside the throne itself. A wide cascading stairway led down from the throne to the plaza below. This positioning gives the gold-plated ivory throne an imposing and awe-inspiring effect.

As the crowds in the plaza look up to Solomon sitting on the throne, he towers above them. In the opposite direction is a view of the temple of Jehovah that has just been completed. As the citizens of his kingdom look to Solomon for wisdom and direction, Solomon looks toward the temple and Jehovah for direction and wisdom. We see Solomon in regal robes of purple sitting upon his throne in judgment. He is sharing the gift of wisdom with citizens of his kingdom and visitors from around the world. A significantly large crowd has gathered below the ivory throne in the courtyard, listening to Solomon's wisdom. Some of those hearing the proclamations are dressed quite uniquely, far differently than the normal attire of Jerusalem's citizens. Their appearance betrays their station in life. They are dignitaries and men of influence. It also declares their nation of origin as they come from many different parts of the globe. The wisdom of Solomon has spread worldwide. He is famously gifted with great insight and understanding. These travelers also came to see the beauty of his palace and the city of Jerusalem as well as to celebrate a very auspicious moment the following day. The attendees all bring exotic gifts when they come to inquire before the king.

On this occasion, Solomon shares insights concerning a very significant subject. He is instructing everyone assembled about the power of words. Solomon declares, "A wholesome tongue is a tree of life. The heart of the wise teaches his mouth and adds learning to his lips. Pleasant words are as a honeycomb, sweet to the soul and health to the bones." To emphasize the point further, Solomon adds, "A man's belly shall be satisfied with the fruit of his mouth, and with the increase of his lips shall he be filled" Then he cautions everyone, saying, "Death and life are in the power of the tongue, and they that love it shall eat the fruit thereof." He continues for some time, sharing many significant truths about the power of words for both good and evil. Everyone listens with great respect and they receive his wise counsel. Solomon finishes his discourse this day with an admonition. "Guard your heart with all diligence for out of it flows the issues of life."

The king arises from the gilded ivory throne. He makes his way toward his private chambers escorted by royal guards. One of his senior advisors informs him that all the preparations have been made for the dedication of the temple of Jehovah tomorrow. Solomon is elated! His men have been working on this project for years. The construction has been completed and he will dedicate the temple tomorrow with sacrifices and prayer to Jehovah. He has given clear instructions to his advisors about the preparation of animals and the temple grounds themselves. He is satisfied that all has been prepared. Tomorrow will be an amazing day for the nation of Israel!

As dinner arrives this night in the newly completed palace banquet hall, Solomon entertains the elders of Israel. All the heads of the tribes, the chief leaders of the land, are present. As they feast and rejoice in the presence of the king, Solomon discusses with them the plans for the following day. He informs the group of leaders that all the treasures that his father, King David, had collected and set aside for the temple, including the silver, the gold, and the instruments are among the treasures of the newly completed house of God. Before the feast, Solomon had escorted them through the portions of his new palace where construction was completed. They were extremely impressed with the beauty and grandeur. About a year earlier, he took up residence within this new palace even though construction on other areas will continue for another seven years. Prior to this, he had been residing in the palace of his father across the valley from the city of Jerusalem in the City of David. This new palace is set in very close proximity to the new temple of Jehovah.

At the banquet table, they discuss the upcoming day. Solomon informs the tribal leaders that citizens from all over the world are in the city to celebrate this special day. Members of all the tribes of Israel are present. The priests and the Levites will bring the ark of the covenant, the tabernacle of the congregation, and all the holy vessels that are in the tabernacle with them in a procession, making their way to the temple. A parade of praise will accompany the procession from its beginning in the City of David. This is the location that King David placed the tabernacle many years before. They will cross the valley, walk up the stairway to the new temple of God, and place the ark within the oracle. The tabernacle itself will be placed in storage areas that are below the Temple Mount. Joy is visible on each face as they discuss the plans and the route that will be taken by the procession of priests, Levites, singers, and musicians from the City of David to the new temple. Each leader is given direction and responsibility for his activities on the Day of Dedication. As Solomon prepares to leave the banquet, he has one more important piece of information to get across to those assembled. Solomon reminds everyone about the significance of this temple. Hiram, the Phoenician king, who assisted them with labor and materials and many other world leaders are present to see the unveiling of a temple like no other on earth. Every other temple among the surrounding nations was built to house an idol of some sort. To those people who created it, those idols represented god. The idol was made by man then worshipped by man. The idols live in these temples, but they do not speak, they do not hear, and they have no power. However, Solomon informs them the temple of God erected in Jerusalem is a temple that could never contain the God he serves. He is Jehovah, Yahweh, the Creator, and preserver of life. No image made by man could ever portray His greatness. In fact, we are instructed by the Lord, never to make any image of anything in heaven or earth and bow down to it in worship.

"Tomorrow," Solomon states, "the world will know, as God's presence is revealed, that there truly is a God in heaven! There is only one true God. It is He who delivered our ancestors from oppression in Egypt and freed us from slavery. It is He who parted the Red Sea. It is He who led them through the wilderness in a cloud of His glory by day and a pillar of fire by night. It is Yahweh, our Lord, who gave us this land that was promised to our ancestor, Abraham. This God, Jehovah, will reveal Himself to all tomorrow. Come prepared to worship Him!"

20

Heaven's Doorway

Preparing a place for the presence of God,
Opens our lives to the promise, the provision, and the purpose of God.

Dedication day has arrived. We view in the hologram of heaven that early morning is breaking in the palace. Solomon has slept very little during the night. He informs us that all through the night, he had rehearsed the journey in his mind over the past seven years. He mused about the development on the adjacent Temple Mount as crews of laborers constructed a special temple for Yahweh. The end result is an incredibly beautiful monument to Jehovah and a worship center for all Israel. In the coming days and years, this place will be the core, the heartbeat of all the feasts and celebrations that God had instituted for their nation. Solomon prayed, worshipped, prepared his heart to deliver a message of instruction and blessing for the nation. He will also offer a prayer to Yahweh on the behalf of the nation of Israel. He asked for the Lord of heaven to receive and honor with His presence this temple that they built for Him. Solomon desired to see and experience the presence and the glory of God as they worshipped in this temple.

The king reviews the day's schedule. He is told that the elders of Israel and all the heads of the tribes have assembled in the city of Jerusalem. He is assured that the priests and the Levites are in the City of David, preparing to dismantle the tabernacle for the last time. They are preparing to transfer the ark of the covenant to the temple of God in Jerusalem. He is pleased with all the details in his morning briefing. The singers and instruments are ready. A multitude of people from all over Israel line each street along the processional route. Everyone is prepared, no detail is missed. He is pleased with his competent and loyal staff and leaders. Prior to leaving for today's magnificent celebration, the king desires a few more moments alone. Solomon's chambers are raised at the highest point within the palace complex. A stairway was constructed alongside the wall, leading directly from his balcony to the roof above. Upon the roof of his palace, Solomon has a private observation point that allows him to have a bird's-eye view, over the entire city of Jerusalem. Immediately before him stands the magnificent temple of God bathed in the glow of the morning sun. He remembers the instructions of his father. From another vantage point across the valley, King David spoke to him of the desire that he had to build a temple for Jehovah. Many times over the last years of his life, King David seated himself across from his son and heir as they looked at this once barren location. They would discuss the plans and preparations for the very temple that he is now viewing. For the first few years of its construction, Solomon observed progress each day from the same vantage point he and his father used so many years before. His father's dream became his dream, and Solomon watched it come to life before him.

During the past year, since moving into his newly constructed palace, Solomon had a much closer view of the daily progress on the Temple Mount. Even though he often visited the construction site and observed in detail the daily transformations as the temple was being erected, he loved the overall view from this private rooftop vantage point. From this position, it seemed to put everything in proper perspective. As he is overlooking the temple, Solomon shares a personal request of the Lord. He asks Jehovah to display His glory this day. He desires that his generation will see the Shekinah glory of the Lord that his ancestors had seen in the wilderness. He desires that they will see the fire of God fall from heaven and consume the sacrifice. This will be a sign to all that the presence and the power of Jehovah has anointed and received this temple as the place where His glory and power would reside on earth. Having finished his time of prayer, Solomon, with a prepared heart and mind, walks down the steps through his private chambers and into the purpose God has for him on this day. He walks out in faith, he walks out in expectation, and he walks out overflowing with great joy.

The scene within the hologram of heaven now changes and transports us to the City of David. We see the last moments of the tabernacle's use by the Israelites. This place, whose plan and directions for use, had been given to Moses by Jehovah on Mount Sinai. This tabernacle, which housed the ark of the covenant with the tablets of stone written by the finger of God, will now be dismantled for the last time. During forty years in the wilderness, as God birthed a nation and led them by His hand, this tabernacle had been in the center of the camp. It is above the mercy seat in the holy of holies of this tabernacle that God would appear in a cloud by day and a pillar of fire by night. It was in this tabernacle that God would meet with and speak to Moses.

An era has ended. A new day has come.

As the Levites first disassemble the outer court walls, we see directly behind the entrance is the brazen altar that was used for many years as the place of sacrifice for sin. The blood of pure, innocent lambs, rams, and bulls are poured out upon the ground near it. This was a necessary penalty to cover man's sin. Parts of their bodies were burned on this altar, speaking of the judgment by death and fire required for man's sin. This altar that traveled with them will be used no more. On the Temple Mount in the city of Jerusalem, there is a new and much larger brazen altar. Hundreds of years before, their ancestor Abraham had been willing to sacrifice his son of promise Isaac on this very mount. For years to come, beginning on this Dedication Day, a new altar will be used. The sacrifices offered in accordance with God's instruction back in the garden of Eden will be offered upon this new altar to Jehovah. *An era has ended. A new day has come.*

Beyond the brazen altar, some of the Levites are clad in white garments as they are dismantling the bronze laver. This laver was made from the bronze mirrors supplied by the women of Israel when offerings were given to build the tabernacle and instruments in the wilderness. It was formed into the shape of a large reservoir or bowl containing water. This has been a place of cleansing for the priests for many years. Here they would wash their hands and feet before they entered the tabernacle's holy place or worked in any service for the Lord within His tabernacle. Inside the new temple courtyard, a laver of much greater size and volume has been designed and produced. It is referred to, as a Molten Sea. The purpose is the same, however, this laver will be used by a much greater number of priests as they wash their hands and feet in preparation for service. This Molten Sea contains enough water for three thousand baths. It sets up above the ground on the hindquarters of twelve bronze oxen. Three oxen face each direction—north, south, east, and west—as their hindquarters meet below the Molten Sea. They act as supports for its weight. The brazen oxen are several steps above the courtyard of the temple. The Molten Sea is in the form of a cup with a lip resembling the lily flower. Water from the Molten Sea flows under the cup onto the base then down a few steps into a wide area around its base with smaller reservoirs. These reservoirs collect the water and are low enough for the priests to comfortably reach into as they bathe their hands and their feet. In addition to the Molten Sea, Solomon also fashioned ten bronze lavers. Each laver contained forty baths. These lavers are set in containers in the shape of a cart, each with four bronze wheels. The brass sides of the carts are engraved with the images of cherubim, lions, and palm trees. These lavers are placed on either side of the temple, five on one side and five on the other. However, these lavers are not to be used by the priest to bathe themselves. These lavers are used to bathe the sacrifices being offered as burnt offerings. Everything is being prepared to provide for a great increase in the number of individuals; who will fellowship with the Lord through the covenant sacrifices. *An era has ended. A new day has come.*

As the Levites continue their work of dismantling the tabernacle for the very last time, we see the coverings over the tabernacle itself being removed. First, they remove the unattractive, waterproof outer layer of badger skins. This reveals another waterproof covering underneath made of ram skins dyed red. As this second layer is removed, we see a black covering of woven goat's hair and directly underneath it is the impressive interior of the tabernacle. This inner covering is of fine twined linen dyed blue, purple, and scarlet. The colors were used to embroider the images of cherubim on the curtains. The images of these beings appear very similar to those who surround the throne of God in heaven. This covering and the veil or curtain that separates the tabernacle into two rooms have great similarity in design. Finally, we see the articles inside: a gold-plated wooden table of shewbread, a beaten golden candlestick and a gold-plated table with incense. These were in the first and larger of the two rooms. In the second and smaller of the rooms, we see the golden ark of the covenant containing the tablets of stone. The covering of beaten gold cherubim resting on top of the ark itself glisten in the morning sun. This covenant box looks so similar to the golden container we have been viewing before the throne of God. The only item from the tabernacle taken into the new temple is the ark of the covenant.

An era has ended. A new day has come. However,
the Covenant will always remain!

The hologram of heaven dissolves before us for a few moments as the father of love instructs the family in heaven. He reminds us of the promise to Abraham and the fulfilment before our eyes. Abraham's family traveled to Egypt, were enslaved, but then delivered four hundred years later. They came out with great riches, He reminds us just as He had said to Abraham. He met with Moses in the wilderness and used him to lead them by the hand. He gave them the promised land. Even when they rebelled, doubted, and tried His patience with their lack of faith and gratitude, our Father showed mercy and grace. Regardless of all their sins and failures at this point and their disobedience to fulfill their part of the covenant, when they turned from their sin and approached in faith through the way of covenant sacrifice, He heard their prayer and delivered them by His Hand. Our loving heavenly Father informs us that the wandering is over. A new opportunity is being presented to His people. He will make Himself known at this time in the city that He chose out of all the cities on the earth to place His name. There are many significant covenant issues yet to be resolved in the coming years according to the Father. The issue will be settled once and for all on Mount Moriah!

As the images of Jerusalem reappear in the hologram before us, we merge with the narrative. Priests and Levites are proceeding along the streets of Jerusalem. At the head of the procession are singers and dancers with cymbals, psalteries, and harp praising the Lord. They are followed by four priests carrying the ark of the covenant. Two long golden staves are slipped through gold rings attached to the ark. The priests alone have permission to carry it this way. No one may touch the ark itself or they will die. Very few individuals have ever seen the ark of the covenant. It is normally hidden from view. Once it is placed inside the temple today, no one except the high priest may see it again for hundreds of years. Those lining the streets as the ark passes by know this. This is a once-in-a-lifetime, perhaps even a once-in-a-millennium, opportunity! Everyone is in awe as they view what few on earth ever will. When the ark was inside the tabernacle during their wilderness wanderings, it was always shrouded from view behind a veil and overshadowed by the presence of God. It was only viewed when they broke camp and traveled.

Knowing this fact, the children of Israel have come from every corner of the kingdom to view this remarkable sight. Some have traveled from all corners of the world for this momentous Day of Dedication. The crowd also includes dignitaries and visiting foreigners who have heard so much about the power of the God of Israel. As the ark passes by, some have tears of joy and worship; others look prayerfully and longingly; and others are shouting, singing, or praising loudly. A tremendous outpour of emotions in worship, love, and praise rings throughout the entire city of Jerusalem. There are always some skeptics mingled in, but today they are by far in the minority. As the priests bearing the ark close in toward the Temple Mount, we see huge crowds packed into every corner around the temple grounds. King Solomon has arrived, flanked by the high priest, leaders of tribes, and many priests and Levites, awaiting the ark's arrival. In the massive temple courtyard surrounded by towering limestone walls, there is barely an inch of open space. One lane is held clear by priests and Levites on either side forming a pathway to carry the ark of the covenant through the courtyard and into the temple of Jehovah. We hear the crescendo of praise building as the ark approaches the entrance to the courtyard.

Solomon is awed by his view of this incredible moment. He is on a raised, bronze platform in the middle of the courtyard. Later, the king will give his address to the crowds, once the Ark has been placed in the oracle of the temple. Solomon watches the singers, dancers, and musicians as they lead the way into the crowded assembly. Directly behind them, the golden ark glows brilliantly in the bright sunlit skies. Slowly, the priests make their way through the open doorway to the temple courtyard as thunderous roars of excitement pour from the voices of God's people. The music and rejoicing mingle in powerful expressions of praise. Slowly, the procession passes the brazen altar that is raised well above the courtyard flooring. Every year on the Day of Atonement from this year forward, a sacrifice will be made upon this new brazen altar. Its blood will be sprinkled on the golden mercy seat that is passing by right now. As a result, God in heaven will cover the sins of Israel for another year. This act is done in anticipation of a greater sacrifice that will one day take place in this very city. Now the ark is passing by the Molten Sea, moving toward the magnificent temple just beyond. This imposing temple is constructed of massive limestone, quarried and hewn into the proper dimension, transported to the Temple Mount, and laid in its unique place as the walls were constructed. The dimensions of the two-room interior is approximately ninety feet long by thirty feet wide and approximately forty-five feet high. The temple faced east and the entrance to the courtyard was on the east side. On the exterior wall along three sides are additional chambers three stories high. Narrow limestone supports are laid against the exterior wall for the beams to rest upon so that nothing was fastened into the wall of the temple itself. Winding stairs lead up from one chamber to another. On the exterior of the temple is a beautiful porch of limestone twenty feet by twenty feet against the east side at the entrance and large, bifolding olive wood doors. These doors are carved in relief with images upon them of cherubim, palm trees, and open flowers. The doors are overlaid with pure gold. In front of the porch on either side are two massive wood columns, carved and then overlaid with gold as well. The top is carved to look like open lilies. As the ark approached the porch, the midmorning sun is shining brightly. The golden doors folded open and the golden columns glow in its light, as does the ark of the covenant on this auspicious day.

The priests carrying the ark are now entering the first interior room. This holy place is sixty feet long by thirty feet wide. The limestone walls are lined and sealed with wood from cedar trees, as are the beams and the ceiling. The interior floor is also made of wood from fir trees. Nothing stone is visible at all from the interior. High up on the walls are narrow rectangular windows for light. We view amazing carved designs of palm trees, cherubim, and open flowers all throughout the room. The floor, walls, and ceiling have all been overlaid with pure gold and are adorned or enhanced with many precious jewels. Light streams in through openings in the windows above and through the doorway, the ark has just passed through. The view is stunning! Pure gold and jewels are everywhere with additional glowing light from ten golden candlesticks lining either side of the room. Day and night, this holy place will be filled with a gleaming richness and beauty! Making their way toward the second interior room, they pass by gold-plated wooden tables for shewbread and then another gold-plated table with a golden vessel upon it. Incense is burning within this vessel, and the aroma is absolutely divine! The oracle, the sacred resting place for the ark of the covenant, and the doorway to the glory of God's presence is raised high above the first room with gold-plated stairs. The interior of this second room is just behind gilded wooden doors, bearing similarity to those we passed entering the holy place. We see the entire oracle is constructed of carved wood and overlaid with pure gold as well. There are two massive cherubim carved of olive wood and also gilded within this smaller chamber. The cherubim's broad wings stretch to reach on one side the interior wall and touch wings with the other cherub on the other side. Their wings span the entire room within the oracle. Every exposed surface in the oracle, this holy of holies, is wood overlaid with the finest of gold. The doors, walls, floor, ceiling, and the cherubim all completely covered with the most precious substance on earth—pure gold!

As the priests are carrying the ark of the covenant, we enter the oracle. It is increasingly difficult to see and maneuver; because as they put the ark beneath the outstretched wings of the cherubim, a heavy mist appears to obstruct our view. Priests assisting in the transfer can barely stand. A deep, dynamic, and powerful presence of the Lord is entering the temple as the Lord graces this place with His presence. Every one of the priests are now finding their way out of the holy place. In the courtyard, Levites, singers, musicians dressed in white linen, and trumpeters playing the shofar raise the call to worship. We hear them play cymbals and many other musical instruments as well. As they begin to praise the Lord, saying, "For He is good, for His mercy endures forever!" The house of the Lord, the temple of Jehovah is enshrouded in God's glory completely, making it impossible for the priests to do any of their ministry and service within the house of the Lord. As we experience this spectacle through the hologram of heaven, the glory cloud that has filled the temple of God bears resemblance to the Shekinah glory cloud around the Father's throne here in heaven. It appears as though God the Father set up an earthly residence in Jerusalem as well. There is a cloud of glory, rising above the oracle of the temple of God in the likeness of the cloud that led the Israelites through the wilderness many years before. It was the presence of God leading them to this land.

Solomon, the king of Israel, stepped to the dais. From this platform above the assembled throng, he began to speak. His initial act, his first words spoken were of acknowledgment and blessing. He turned from a view of the temple, now filled with God's presence, to face the assembly of Israelites. As he raised his hands toward them, he blessed them in the name of the Lord God of Israel. In this blessing, Solomon proclaimed the faithfulness of God to his father, King David, and to the nation of Israel. He declared that there is no God like our God! One who is alive, a God who hears and answers prayer. He recited the interventions of God in the history of their family and nation. Solomon continued on to say that the Lord God of Israel could not be contained within this temple. Even the heavens themselves cannot contain him! But the king declares that God will meet them here in this place of worship and prayer. This place is a direct pathway to heaven for those who truly seek not only for the children of Israel, but it will be a place where people from all nations who seek Him can contact the living God! This will be called a house of prayer for all nations.

Prior to the ark's arrival at the temple, sacrifices had been prepared for Solomon and all the people. The first sacrificial offerings were already upon the altar, but the fire had not been lit to burn them. Following the blessing of the nation, Solomon turned to the temple and offered a prayer of supplication to the Lord. He asked the Lord to keep His eyes upon this house day and night, the place where He placed His name. He petitioned the Lord to hear his prayers and the prayers of the people. Solomon prayed that as the Lord heard the prayers offered in this place, He would truly hear from his dwelling place in heaven and Solomon asked the Lord that when He hears, "Please forgive." Many of the covenant promises, as well as blessings and curses. were recited before the Lord that day. A pathway between God in heaven and man on earth is opened upon this Temple Mount. Finishing his prayer, Solomon boldly prayed. "Arise, O Lord God, into thy resting place, thou, and the ark of thy strength: let thy priests, O Lord God, be clothed with salvation, and let thy saints rejoice in goodness" (2 Chron. 6:41, KJV).

When the prayer ended, "the fire of God came down from heaven, and consumed the burnt offering and the sacrifices; and the glory of the Lord filled the house" (2 Chron. 7:1, KJV). What an incredible display of power we have just witnessed. The fire of God from the throne of God in heaven above was flashing instantly in all-consuming power upon the brazen altar. This powerful demonstration was a resounding "yes" from the Lord God of heaven to the prayers of an anointed man on earth. This display of heavenly fire was so supernatural and dynamic that as the fire fell and the glory of God appeared upon the temple, everyone in the assembly fell prostrate before the Lord, bowing before their maker. They declared that, "God is good! His mercy endures forever!"

To sanctify the new brazen altar to atone for the sins of the nation that day and each day following for seven days total, sacrifices were continually made to sanctify the altar. So many were bringing their offerings for sacrifice, having the desire to renew their commitments to Jehovah that a second altar was sanctified on which they would offer some of the smaller offerings. During the seven days of feasting and offering sacrifices to the Lord, all the people rejoiced in God's goodness, His presence, and His power. They recited to each other and to their children the miraculous interventions of God in the life of their families and nation. The pinnacle of it all, the greatest of blessings, is that the God of heaven, the Creator of life, has now made His earthly home in Jerusalem. As Solomon released everyone to go home to their cities, following the weeklong festival, they left with joy and thanksgiving in their hearts!

As the hologram of heaven slowly dissolves, we see thankful believers from every area of Israel, making their way home. We rejoice with them at the wonder of God's presence now situated in His temple. He is there among His people.

A doorway to heaven is now open on earth.

WHAT'S COMING!

SHEPHERDING A CHILD'S HEART SEMINAR

April 17-18TH

Join us as we welcome Dr. Tedd Trip for the Shepherding a Child's Heart Seminar from Friday to Saturday. For more information or to register, visit RedeemerPV.com/events

SAVE THESE DATES:

JAX United and the Icemen | March 6, 7PM

Easter Sunday | April 12

GROWTH TRACK

STEP ONE | Today, 12PM Come learn more about Redeemer Church! Step One is about belonging. Lunch and childcare are provided.

SUNDAY SCHOOL

Sundays at 9AM

Join us for adult Sunday school.

DOWNLOAD THE APP

Text "RedeemerPV App" to 77977 to download our church app.

CHURCH PRAYER FOCUS

Trinity Church

Pray for their Buddy Team Ministry and their desire for people of all ages with special needs to feel welcomed, loved and included in Sunday Services. Each person is paired with a buddy as they worship and experience God's love.

John 17:20-21   ONE CHURCH, ONE BODY

SERMON NOTES

_____
_____
_____
_____
_____
_____
_____
_____
_____
_____
_____
_____
_____
_____
_____
_____
_____

KEY POINTS

_____
_____
_____
_____

21

From Grace to Disgrace

From glory and grace, to shame and disgrace
when men don't seek His face.

Here in the throne room, Solomon remains standing as *Story Time in Heaven* continues. In the presence of our heavenly Father and the saints of all ages, Solomon has a somber confession to make. We see him look toward the Father of love upon His throne and then to the saints gathered in the throne room of heaven. In the presence of great witnesses, Solomon confirms to everyone present that it was the Lord who had given to him wisdom, riches, and honor in his life. The Lord of heaven and earth had blessed him above all others before or after him. Following the dedication of the temple of God that we have just witnessed God Himself appeared to Solomon.

The Father of love, the God of Israel promised to bless both King Solomon and his posterity if he continued following the Lord with all his heart. The God of Israel had opened a doorway to blessing, forgiveness, prayer, and fellowship if they would offer the prescribed sacrifices for the sins of the people here in Jerusalem. This was the place God chose to reveal himself and where the blood covenant sacrifices were to be offered in faith. This place, for the remainder of time, will hold great significance. The Lord also declared that if he turned aside to other gods and stopped following the Lord, great devastation and trouble would be brought upon his family and his nation. Just as on Mount Gerizim where the blessings of the covenant of love were pronounced and on Mount Ebal where curses for turning away from the covenant were recited, so here in Jerusalem with the people of Israel and then individually with King Solomon were the blessing and curses pronounced. Access to a relationship with God the Father, the Creator, since the first day of man's sin in the garden of Eden, has always been predicated upon the covenant of love and the sacrificial offerings. There has always been one basis for a relationship with the God of heaven. Without the shedding of blood, there is no remission, release, or forgiveness of sin.

"Sadly," King Solomon continues, "I failed in life in so many different ways. Though I had been given wisdom, I also had a divided heart. I was not content just to know goodness and truth. I was not satisfied to know only what was wise and right. But I was enticed, much like our ancestor Eve in the garden of Eden. I wanted to know not only good and truth, but I desired to know foolishness. I ached to know about madness and folly. I had a passion to experience the pleasures of the forbidden fruit of lust. I had the urge to expose myself to the effects of wine and alcohol. I craved to experience the feelings of drunkenness. Would it bring happiness, laughter, and mirth? How would I act when drunk? Would I act foolish and wild or somber and sullen? I had a fondness for music of every kind and style. The worship music of the psalms had always been my delight, but I eventually embraced music that did not honor Jehovah. By their lyrics and rhythm, this music from the ungodly nations around us promoted lust and evil desires. I had huge ambitions to make a name for myself by building great edifices that would honor my time as king of Israel. All over the nation, especially in Jerusalem, I built many structures. I enlarged my palace to allow room for the many wives I acquired from all the nations around Israel. I eventually constructed a huge harem within my palace. In total, I had seven hundred wives and three hundred mistresses. I indulged in all their sinful practices. I became acquainted with their gods and became involved in their devilish, sensual, and evil worship styles. I sought to know about their gods and built many worship centers for these foreign wives and their gods. All the high places on the hills surrounding Jerusalem were gradually filled with worship places. Here my wives and I worshipped the gods of men's fashion and design. These were gods made of wood or carved in stone and had images of things in the heavens or on earth. These gods had mouths but they did not speak, eyes but could not see, and ears but could not hear. They also had feet but could not move and hands that could not touch. They were the creation of man. We deceived ourselves in worshipping and serving creatures of our own design rather than the Creator of Life!

I designed elaborate gardens and orchards and planted many fruit-bearing trees. I accumulated great amounts of gold, silver, and treasures of every kind. Whatever my eyes desired, I went after. I did not withhold my heart from any pleasure or joy. I did not deny my flesh any of its cravings. I turned away from the pursuit of the knowledge and wisdom of God, but embraced the wicked wisdom of the world. What a disaster this was!" he confesses. Solomon goes on to say that by opening his heart to evil, he became controlled by the same alien invader that had enticed Eve in the garden. "After years of indulgence and debauchery, I looked around at all that I had done, all that I had seen, and all that I had learned in life, and *all was vanity.* I only lived for myself. I was pretentious, vain, conceited, and selfish! The entirety of my life's work was useless, futile. My heart was empty. My life, my home, my city, and my kingdom was filled with evil, not the presence of God. My life, filled with so much promise at the start, was now wasted in total vanity. My wives were constantly in conflict with each other. This brought great vexation to my spirit. All that I had acquired, I now realized, would be left behind to others. Nothing would leave this world with me when I died. All the accumulation of wealth was a wasted effort!" Solomon adds, "The Lord is merciful. He is gracious, He is faithful! The Lord is long-suffering, not willing that any should perish." He declares that in the end he returned to Jehovah and to the blood covenant. These sacrifices covered his sins, which were many. He then completed his narration with an admonition, one that he had left in writing on earth for all who would succeed him. He instructs everyone to remember their Creator while they are young and urges them not waste their lives in sinful actions as he had done. He reminded all that we are made of dust and to dust our bodies will return, however, our spirit will answer to our Maker.

The Father has everything in our lives recorded. He finishes with this statement, "Fear God, and keep His commandments: for this is the whole duty of man."

Solomon's confession stuns us! In the hologram of heaven, we are watching his amorous, evil, and wicked actions. As observers on this imaginary journey to heaven, we wonder how Solomon even made it here to heaven. Our answer comes in King Solomon's concluding statements. Near the end of his life, he realized his vanity, foolishness, and evil ways. He informs us that he repented before the Lord. He went by the way of blood covenant sacrifice to the temple of God. He asked the only true and wise God, the Creator of the universe to forgive him. Hearing the story of Solomon, the pinnacle of wisdom and worship in the presence of God and his great work in building the temple of God then his fall and final state gives us pause to contemplate. Those of us who are visiting this celestial city in our imagination know of many who started well and then faltered in their walk with God on earth. They remain, to this day, estranged from God. Solomon's story gives us hope that when we have completed this imaginary excursion to heaven, we will be able to communicate with them that *a second chance is available*. All is not lost if breath remains in their body!

We begin to thank and praise God because He is long-suffering, patient, merciful, and gracious! We join in to sing along with heaven's citizens as they pour from their hearts in one of the great hymns of the faith, "Great is thy Faithfulness. Morning by morning, new mercies I see!" In story after heavenly story, the family of God declares, "How great is our God!" As we finish the chorus, looking about in the vast grandstand of heaven, we observe many leaving the throne room of the Father and heading out to the golden avenues of heaven. It is obvious that there is a pause in the family story. We begin an intermission for a designed purpose. We follow the multitudes as they discuss among themselves the revelations that we all heard. There have been so many twists and turns during the family history. Each citizen of heaven discusses with those around them details of the unique and wonderful stories we have been experiencing as every story glorifies the Father of Love.

Our hearts sense something a little unusual, even surprising—a beautiful and new awareness. We acknowledge something deep and personal as we move about in this glorious place called heaven. We have become cognizant of a feeling—no, much more than a feeling, a fact! Though we are just visiting heaven in our imagination, *we are somehow at home* in this beautiful city. Indeed, we feel comfortable and welcome; even in the very throne room of heaven. *Wow!* This revelation in our hearts fills us with wonder. In the very seat of power—not only on earth and the universe, but for all of eternity—we are as at home in this place of power as a child on his Father's knee. Heaven is a wonderful place! I had no idea before embarking on this adventure, that I would feel so comfortable and relaxed in God's presence. I had no idea that the throne room of the universe, the very seat of power where the fullness of God's presence and glory dwells, would be such a welcoming, joyful and love-filled atmosphere.

New arrivals from all over the earth have the same reaction and experience. We see them constantly arriving. Once their life on earth has ended, those who believe are instantly transported by their guardian angel to this place. As they arrive, the greetings of love are genuine, sincere, and honest. I remember something that the psalmist said many, many years ago. He said, "How amiable are thy tabernacles, Oh Lord" or in my vernacular, "How friendly and pleasant is the place where God dwells." Truly, this abode of God's people, this city filled with redeemed saints, and this place where the love of God rules supreme is such an amiable and happy place! Everyone here is cordial, kind and loving. Everyone receives each other, as the Father of Love has received them. We acknowledge that the citizens of this celestial city are easy to interact and get along with because the love of God flows from one heart to another, unhindered by doubt, fear, or any other negative attitude.

No sin, no fear is ever allowed in the celestial city.

During this intermission, we are carried in spirit outside the city. As we move into the vast reaches of eternity, the heavenly city appears even larger from this vantage point. How happy we are that so many are moving into this blissful, eternal home. As we move out of the celestial city and into the openness of eternity, we are overwhelmed with its vastness. Heaven is but a glow in the distance as we move farther and farther away into the realm of eternity, into the emptiness of total darkness and silence. The awareness of infinity, a consciousness of never-ending space, envelops us. This place in eternity has no view of heaven, earth, or the universe—nothing at all. Words cannot describe the depth, the openness, and the distances that we experience as these impressions bombard our senses. Yet we are not in fear because we have the knowledge and the sense within our spirits; that even though nothing else seems to inhabit the unending spaces of eternity, we still feel the presence of the Father deeply. He inhabits all of eternity. Everywhere we are, He is! As we become conscious of this truth, we know that even here where nothing exists, it is but a place where the word of God could create even more amazing worlds.

The blackness of eternity is but a canvas for
the artistry and creativity of God.
One word from His lips could transform this entire
deep and dark dimension. Amazing!

As we journey through this vast eternal space, the universe our Father created comes into view. We glide into the majestic view of billions of galaxies, each composed of millions of stars and planets. As we circle the stars, we understand that every galaxy, every star, and every planet is incredibly unique! They are purposely placed in the positions and orbits that they maintain, as does everything else in the universe that the Creator has designed. Each galaxy, star, and planet is named and given its purpose by God Himself!! *The designs that form constellations painted by the brushstrokes of God on the parchment of space truly displays His glory!*

On this delightful and exhilarating cruise through the galaxies, we are seeing and experiencing sights that have never been viewed by the human eye. Even with the most powerful telescopes on earth or even those stationed outside of the earth's atmosphere, man is unable to peer into the depths of space that we are now viewing. Incredible, awe-inspiring, and magnificent is the Father of Love and His great power As we glide swiftly through the universe, the knowledge that this is all designed, held together, and maintained by the power of God's words alone is astounding! There is a purpose in this journey through the universe during our intermission in heaven. The spirit of our imagination is leading us to a place outside of heaven within the universe. This is a place that neither we nor anyone else on earth has ever seen before. We are not certain at this point if the location is on another planet or perhaps some place within the bowels of the earth itself. It seems to me to be the latter. We are drawn to it in our imagination. From quite a distance away, strange noises begin to reach our ear. These unusual sounds increase in volume as we are approaching the area, and their somber and striking tones are very troubling. They seem to be cries of discontent, fear, and pain. We hear the groaning of people in great sorrow and sadness. As we arrive at the scene, we are unable to initially identify any faces. The land that we have entered appears to be a divided place. There are two very expansive areas with vast spaces, large enough for millions of spirits to dwell within. As we view these two broad, spread-out areas, we observe a very large, impassable gulf of space separating the two regions. The entire area on both sides of the gulf seems to be encircled with large fences and a huge locked gate. There are no bridges or passageways in which a person could traverse from one side to the other.

Something about this vision seems very odd. One side is exquisitely beautiful. It appears to be a flowered oasis. There is color, beauty, peace, and tranquility. This side of the gulf would be a delight to dwell in. It is a little slice of heaven; in fact, this garden of beauty is very similar to Adam's description of the garden of Eden. There are trees, flowers, meadows, and crystal clear streams bubbling up from beneath the surface. These streams then meander in a winding fashion into beautiful ponds dotting the landscape. The aroma of the flora blossoming in beauty along the banks and in the meadows is divine! Everything about this area exudes comfort, joy, and relaxation. We smile as we observe this fragrant and peaceful area, yet we are perplexed at the same time. A wonderful and lovely oasis such as this should be filled to overflowing, however, it is entirely empty—an uninhabited yet delightful realm.

The other side of the gulf is exactly the opposite in appearance. This area is like a desert—hot, uncomfortable, stressful, and sorrowful—without water or vegetation. The stench of this vast area is rank and repulsive. We smell only the awful odor of death and rot. Filthy, dusty dirt fills the atmosphere. The stink of this place reminds us of burning sulfur or rotten eggs. Within the dry, burning heat and rancid smell of this miserable place, we are shocked to behold multitudes of people, millions upon millions. The numbers appear to be growing rapidly. Others are entering this tormented place in constant flow. The calamitous plight of these beings is such a disturbing sight, augmented by the fact that while so many are entering here, no one is entering the paradise on the other side of the gulf. The individuals residing in this desert place appear tormented, thirsty, fearful, and totally bereft of hope. Yet there is a presence of evil that we sense here, a wickedness and a total lack of love or peace. We discern that this evil has penetrated these tormented souls completely. Who are these individuals? How did they ever get into this predicament? Why are they not on the other side of the gulf? They can see the beautiful oasis from where they are, but somehow they have no ability to get to the other side. We are not given the answer at this time, but we have a distinct impression, that we were led here by the spirit of our imagination for a reason. We will learn the answer to our questions. Of this, I am certain.

22

The Father's Heart Exposed

Swiftly, instantly, and without warning!

In a phenomenal display of supernatural power, we have been transported into the celestial city. What an incredible rush! We have just experienced unimaginable, split-second speed. Quicker than the blink of an eye and faster than the speed of light, we moved from the sight of sorrow into the presence of heaven's glory. It was instantaneous transfer. *Wow!* We felt as though a gigantic magnet in heaven drew us with incomprehensible speed. What a breathtaking and inspiring manifestation of God's power! As we catch our breath, we know we have just experienced the speed in which a soul and spirit moves from earth to glory. When a believer sheds the robe of flesh, this is how quickly they are ushered into heaven's portals by their guardian angels. What rapture, what pleasure, and what delight! I understand more fully now what the Apostle Paul declared, when he wrote "to be absent from the body is to be present with the Lord."

Smiling, we have the distinct impression that intermission is over! We have been brought back to the heavenly city just in time to hear the Father of love as He sends out a call to heaven's family to assemble in the throne room. As we make our joyful way toward the stadium of heaven, our hearts are full of excitement and genuine praise as we ponder the wonder and glory of our amazing heavenly Father. We have questions in our minds as well but somehow know that the answers will come. The spirit in our imagination has guided us on this journey. We know God has a purpose in all that has taken place. During this fantastic excursion to heaven, millions of saints from all ages are moving into their own unique and personal positions in the presence of the king. We receive new revelations and gain greater understanding as we surveil the scene. One constant in heaven is great order and complete unity. We see each citizen returning to their same unique place in the throne room. Each seems to understand their individual place and function as a part of the whole. All of heaven operates smoothly like one perfectly functioning body.

This power center for earth and heaven and all in between is constantly abuzz with intricate and harmonious activity, regardless of whether an assembly has been called or has paused for an intermission. This activity is never a distraction to the story, but simply the normal functions of the seat and source of power for the entire universe! While we are enjoying *Story Time in Heaven* with our heavenly family, our loving Father is engaged with these activities and with the story line as He is connecting with the family in heaven. However, at the very same time, He is always engaged in communication with individuals on earth. Believers on earth are reaching by the spirit into heavens portals...directly to the Throne of Grace. We see that they are coming by way of covenant and approaching the Father by referring to the blood, the scarlet liquid that is flowing over the golden container positioned directly before the Father's throne. Each one who appears before him comes by faith in the promise of God and in His glorious Son. The Father is never overwhelmed by the volume of requests. We sense His great joy as He is releasing blessings upon His children through His power-filled words.

Often, the Father dispatches angels to become involved in the affairs of men. Messages, it appears, are transmitted through Gabriel, a glorious and impressive leader among angels. Strong warrior angels are dispatched at the Father's direction by the Archangel Michael to the legions under his command. We have many questions about how everything operates in this spiritual heavenly realm. In our spirits, we feel this first journey to heaven will not answer all our questions on that subject, but we desire to come back and learn more in succeeding adventures. Many questions fill our minds. In our spirits, we sense that the subject of one of our next imaginary journeys to *Story Time in Heaven* may include heavenly warfare and the battle of the ages. Our minds are drawn back from their wandering and curious way by melodic sounds of praise. We hear the harmonious strains of heaven's orchestra as they worship lovingly. Saints of all ages join the symphony, blending in colorful harmony and expressing in song and dance the love they all feel for the Father. We join in from our hearts. Everything else around us dims as the magnificent rainbow of color glows and reflects in the Shekinah glory cloud surrounding the Father's throne. Millions of arms are raised in worship toward the Father and the Son. Others bow in adoration or lay prostrate before God's throne. In moments like these, the depths of God's love flowing between the Father, the Son, and the family, is so deep, so rich, and so sweet. Enthroned in this worship and praise, the Father and the Son express to us the love They have for the entire family. We sense the Father has much to share. He called us to this assembly to resume the family story, and so *Story Time in Heaven* continues. Our heavenly Father will now address the assembly of saints. He desires to enlighten us with revelations and dynamic truths directly from His heart. During the reign of King Solomon in Israel, the Father reminds us that He placed His name and blessing on the city of Jerusalem and the temple of God that Solomon constructed. He declared Himself to be the God of Israel, sent the glory of His presence to inhabit the temple, and sent fire from heaven to consume the covenant sacrifice, reestablishing the blood covenant of love between the God of Israel and its people. However, we heard about the tragic failure and the errors that he made from the lips of King Solomon himself. Solomon stopped worshipping the Lord. He chose rather to create and serve other gods of this world.

Our Father pauses for a long, weighty moment. The Father of love and the Son of God, the Living Word, sincerely and soberly directs us to be very attentive. The Lord of heaven and earth instructs us to focus our minds, to listen closely, and to open our souls to understand. Viewing from the portals of heaven, we clearly get the impression something very significant is about to be revealed. We sense that what is about to be disclosed will be very consequential.

It is foundational and critical for all to know and understand our Father's ways. When this series of stories was initiated; the Father reminds us, that He laid out the facts regarding the origin of all life. In the beginning, He alone existed. All life flowed from Him. His heart of Love was so full. As we experience this journey, He is, in essence, *love* itself!! Our Father of love desired to create a family to share His love and power with them. He desired children, offspring that would be like Him. These descendants were to bear His image and likeness. God's offspring were to walk in His love and power. God's family members were created to replicate and reflect their Father's character and display the glory of His grace throughout the ages yet to come. They were to rule and reign with the Son of God for all eternity.

We are reminded of the creation of Adam and the birth of God's first earthly son. The Father and His son Adam visit in the garden each day, and the fellowship was beautiful. Adam was given the *power of choice*. He was not made to be a robot, but a son. Adam was given authority by the Father. Very little restriction was placed upon him, except the instruction to not eat of the tree of the knowledge of good and evil. *Within the power of choice, man's greatest power is the glory and the conundrum of the ages.* The power of choice gives man so much freedom and control over his life. However, Adam *was not* given the authority to choose evil or rebellion. The power of choice gives man *delegated* power from the Father of love. Having the ability by choice to do an evil act does not give any man the authority or permission to commit that evil act. Adam was only authorized to act under the direction of the heavenly Father.

Our loving heavenly Father pauses to enlighten us more fully about the puzzling conundrum of the ages. He gently explains that everything in the universe—on earth, among the galaxies, and stars, even here in heaven and in the never-ending reaches of eternity—*operates and functions through the power of His words.* The vastness of the heavenly bodies in the universe that declare His glory and the earth, with its intricate flow of life that shows His complex handiwork and creativity *are all in sync and are supported by the power of His words. The character, purpose, and power of all things is sustained, maintained, and held together by the power and authority of the words of God alone! There is balance and beauty in all that He has made.* We are then instructed that any step or decision to move outside of the boundaries of God's will, as expressed in His words, brings conflict and takes us entirely out of balance with God and the universe. As an example, the heavenly Father enlightens us that the laws of physics are laws men have discovered and named. However, He reminds us it is He, the heavenly Father, who created, designed, and sustains them. If the law of gravity was to be suspended, if the power of His words were to fail or grow weak for even a few moments, catastrophic damage would take place in the universe. All living creatures would float off the earth and perish. Planets and stars would lose their orbits as crashing and cascading planets and stars collided in thermonuclear explosions. Throughout our earth and universe are many physical laws created and established by God's words. When men discovered the truth of each law and learned to work in harmony with its power, they discover constant results that can be relied upon and harnessed for their good. *Men are simply discovering the potential that has always been inherent within.* This power, order, and constant truth was established by God's word, and it is present in every dimension! When men follow and apply these natural laws, they are often unwittingly following principles established by God's word.

It matters not, whether it is a physical, mental, or spiritual dimension. It matters not whether it is in heaven, in the universe, or in the constant and never-ending reaches of eternity. "There has always been, and shall ever be, only one God," our Father declares. This is not debatable; this is simply truth revealed. It is His word, His will, and His power that is supreme in all dimensions. His children and indeed everything else in all dimensions is designed to live, to move, and to have its existence within the protective boundaries of God's eternal words. His words will never pass away and will never lose their power. Hearing our Father explain these truths fills us with joy. On earth, we know some men struggle as they wrestle in their minds …with the truths our Lord reveals. Faith, trust, and openness of heart and mind is required to understand. From here in heaven's portals, viewing the awesomeness of this scene, there is no doubt at all concerning every detail our Father discloses.

Oh, how my heart aches for a vehicle, a mechanism that would allow others to witness what we are witnessing in our imagination here in heaven this day!

Expanding on the basis of what our heavenly Father just shared, He continues to apply these truths to our family's story. When Adam sinned by disobeying the directives of his Father's words, everyone viewed in the hologram of heaven the swift manner in which discord, disease, and death entered the human family. Because all men were a part of Adam and came from him throughout the ages since, his fallen state of confusion and estrangement from God was passed on to all his posterity. Because of Adam, we all sinned and died spiritually. We all lost fellowship in the spirit with our Father. *Since Adam, all men were born with the tendency to sin.* His descendants were not conceived in Adam's innocent state in the garden before sin. *All his descendants came after the entrance of sin.* He was originally designed to know only that which is good, but through disobedience, he and all his descendants have known both good and evil. The war of good against evil rages on to this day. Adam was also given authority over the earth by the Father. Because of his disobedience, the entire earth was thrown into chaos and confusion.

Our Father explains that when Adam sinned, he positioned himself to be God over his own life. He chose to be the final authority within his own domain. His action was not an innocent, accidental tasting of the wrong fruit by mistake. *It was the abuse of his power to choose.* It was direct disobedience to the Father of love, the Creator and preserver of life! The moment Adam sinned, he died spiritually. The unique life of the spirit, the communion and fellowship with God, his Father, was lost. His soul, mind, will, and emotions were tarnished, defiled, and brought into discord, strife, and division. The war between good and evil for dominance over his life began to rage. He passed this same inner warfare between good and evil to all who succeeded him. The beginning of death and decay began in his body.

Generation after generation, man's life span began to shorten until the Father intervened and allowed seventy or eighty years for most of mankind.

Sin has devastating repercussions!

The Father of Love reminds us that He knows all things before they ever happen. He knew the effect, both positive and negative, of providing man with the power to choose. Knowing what Adam would do, He planned a way back and a way forward for man. He provided a way of forgiveness, a way of cleansing, a way of restoration, a way back to sonship, and a way back to the original purpose for which man was made. We have witnessed story after story, from one generation to the next of covenants between God and man. *From the very beginning, one truth has been known in the earth; whether received or rejected by man...and that truth is: "Without the shedding of blood...there is no remission of sin"* Sin brought death, and the life of all flesh is in the blood. This covenant of love, the blood covenant, does not free men from sin by itself, but does point to the sacrifice of one who would come, the Son of God, the one who would become the second Adam.

As the heavenly Father opens His heart, we hear a wonderful outpouring of love. Our Father begins to share His thoughts as He watched man's struggling and wandering way. The Lord of love describes how His eyes have continually searched to and fro throughout the whole earth. He has been searching every heart throughout the ages and looking for any man or woman with a tender, open or seeking heart. All those who perished without Him did so of their own accord and by their own design. It is not the Father's design that any should perish. He desired to show them His love and their potential if they would open their hearts to the truth. He is the Good Shepherd who seeks His lost sheep. He is the Father who, with extravagant love, watches earnestly down the road, waiting for His wandering son to return. We see in our previous story that no matter how far away he strayed, the Father awaited King Solomon's return. When anyone returned to the covenant of love, there was great rejoicing in heaven! Our Father found many as His eyes searched the earth throughout the ages past. Noah, as we have heard, was used to save the entire species of man. Others whose stories have been displayed before us on the hologram of heaven and indeed multitudes more responded to the word. Each one embraced the covenant of love. They are the souls surrounding us now in the assembly of the saints here in heaven. With each embrace of the covenant, from Adam to Noah, Abraham, Moses, and the nation of Israel, Our Father highlighted more clearly and in great, detail the blessings of obedience to the covenant and the curses of disobedience. He even gave them detailed laws and instructions so that they could follow more surely in His ways. However, within the laws themselves, there was no power for the nature of man to be changed. *Adam's sin stained mankind in both soul and body.*

Our Father proclaims His eternal desire, dream, and purpose from the beginning was much more than to have His family dwell on the earth alone. His desire was to have His children live with Him in heaven, this fantastic place we are visiting in our imagination even now. However, no amount of animal sacrifices could remove the stain of sin from man and open a place for him in heaven. An animal's blood could, when poured out in obedience and faith, cover man's sin and allow God's forgiveness and blessing upon him on the earth, but it could never atone for his sin here in heaven. The rebellion and effects of man's sin must always remain in the realm where man originally dwelt on earth. No sin, no rebellion, nothing outside of perfect harmony with God's word may ever enter heaven. Something far greater and much more powerful was necessary before man could enter the portals of heaven. It is because of this truth, until a better covenant and sacrifice was made, no one entered heaven from the earth. Our Father informs us of a place He prepared for those who worshipped and followed Him under the covenant of love. The Father reminds many of the saints assembled here how they had gone to that place themselves when they died, a place called paradise. We see many saints nod their heads in assent; in fact, every speaker we have heard thus far is acknowledging its truth. Paradise was not in heaven, but still in man's realm within the universe. Within this massive area, our Father informs us He prepared a divided place. There were two vast realms placed in this dimension with a great gulf fixed between them. One area was created in likeness to the garden of Eden; a place to house His children. Inhabitants of this garden were all children of the covenant of love. Here they would wait until the appointed time that He could transfer them to heaven. This place was referred to by the Son of God as Abraham's bosom.

Across the gulf, separating the two realms of this dimension, were placed the souls of those who rejected His love, His covenant, and his family. There is a reckoning day approaching for these wicked and rebellious souls. They can never enter heaven. Our heavenly Father informs us that he established this dimension from the first day of man's sin and of the establishment of the blood covenant, the covenant of love. It was just before this assembly and before experiencing the amazing, exhilarating, journey back to heaven that we had visited paradise. We now understand why paradise is empty and the identity of the multitudes on the other side of the gulf. But we wonder when and how was paradise emptied. What was done that allowed them to enter heaven?

23

Willing Vessels

Be it unto me according to your word.

As we are listening to the Father of love, we are touched deeply by His compassionate heart. We hear our Father recall earth's history from the first day of man's sin all through the entire time of our family story to Solomon and indeed for hundreds of years after. We see displayed on the hologram of heaven one generation after another. In each generation throughout the entire earth, the Father shows us the many ways that he endeavored to call out to man. He used a multitude of means to get man's attention to preserve him from death and to call to their hearts. He used signs in the heavens in every language they were displayed. He displayed signs in the earth and worked miracles by his might. There were many who responded, many who entered the protection of the covenant of love. However, the vast, majority of mankind shunned the Lord of heaven and His plans. In many generations, only a small remnant was responsive to His love. The Shepherd was not sought in return. The Father awaiting His wandering children, often waited in vain. Though not wanting man to perish, their rebellion was deep and real. Men had a propensity to embrace a life of sin. Their fondness for evil and love for earthly, sensual gratification led to this penchant for sin. *Their desire for momentary pleasure drowned out their potential for eternal delight! It suffocated heavenly possibilities, submerging them in the watery grave and lustful grip of present, earthly passions!*

Our Father desired the truth of the blood covenant to be pro-claimed to each society on each continent. Rather than seek its truth from the God of heaven whose blessing they would receive, they perverted and polluted its beauty and truth. When the Lord found anyone willing to receive, He blessed them and prospered their way. He used this as an example to all those around. He wrought miracles for Israel's leaders when they followed His commands. Our Father destroyed their many enemies, often by His hand alone. The stories were told, the facts were true! Yet regardless of all he did, men still drifted on in sin. Prophets spoke God's warning, confirmed by signs from heaven above. Miracles of healing, protection, and intervention confirmed the Lord's unequaled power displayed for all men to see. But for a momentary repentance, man continued his own way to seek. Our Father had seen enough. For four hundred years, He was silent. No prophet, no priest, and no new word from heaven. God knew the stain of sin from Adam penetrated deeply into the core of mankind. It was time to begin anew! Our Father informs us that there was but one way to start over. No man on earth could escape the stain of sin. All of Adam's seed was contaminated by its awful effects. A new Adam was needed, one that would be pure and free from sin. One that would walk in obedience to the Father's com-mands and eventually pay the price for all men's sin.

A decision had been made.

We are now told of a crucial choice that was made in eternity past. In the counsel of heaven in the heart of the Triune God in the infinite foreknowledge of the Holy One even before time began. The Holy Son of God, the eternal Word of heaven would lay aside the power and glory He possessed in eternity at a predetermined time. The only begotten Son of God would put on a robe of flesh and enter the universe as a man. He would limit Himself to walk in the position and authority that the first Adam had before the first day of man's sin. He would submit Himself to walk in obedience under the rule of the Father of love. He would only speak the truth. His words would be light and life. *He would create a new species of man, a species fit not only for earth, but for entrance to heaven as well!*

Now rising before the assembly of heaven and near to the throne of God's Son is a woman with a story to tell. As she begins to relate the story in the hologram of heaven, we are drawn into the scene of a city in Galilee called Nazareth, nearly a thousand years after the time of King David and King Solomon. A young woman of Israel, a descendant of King David and a soul who had a heart for God, is resting in her home and pondering the wonders of the God of Israel. Mary shares with us that all her life, she had been told stories of her ancestor King David and of his glorious victories over Goliath, and many others. She was so proud to be one of his descendants. She read the psalms that he wrote and enjoyed singing them herself. Mary's love for Jehovah was so deep as well. She was thankful in her heart for the promises of the covenant of love. She and her family were very devout in their faith. They endeavored to follow all the instructions of the law. Every year, they would go to Jerusalem for the great festivals and present their offerings before the Lord. Her cousin Elizabeth was even married to a priest named Zacharias! As she lay in her bed on this quiet evening, Mary informs us that she was musing about the wonder of God. She had been betrothed recently to a carpenter in their village, a man named Joseph. He was also a descendant of King David. She pondered her future and her life. She was happy, but Mary also longed for deliverance for her people. Rome had conquered her nation. This powerful and distant country ruled them with an iron rod. Life was sometimes difficult, but she believed for many years that a Messiah would come and deliver the nation from their oppressors. She had hope for Israel. Little did Mary know that in that hour, a momentous and consequential meeting was just ahead.

The scene in the hologram changes to the throne room of heaven at the time Mary was pondering these things. The Father is there with the angels, however, there are no saints in the grandstand of heaven. Our Father is giving a message to Gabriel as he is standing at attention before the presence of God. He tells Gabriel, "It is urgent, give this message to Mary immediately. 'All is prepared. The time has come'!" From the dimension of heaven's throne room to the small room where Mary reposed took but a second of earth's time. It was an immediate transfer from one dimension to another for Gabriel's presence to appear. The angel greets Mary, with a wonderful salutation, a commendation from the Lord of heaven. He tells her she is highly favored by the God of Israel. He informs Mary, "God is with you. You are blessed among women." The appearance of Gabriel and the greeting from heaven surprised and confused Mary. Aware of her confusion, Gabriel instructed Mary not to fear. He assured her that she had found favor with God. He went on to share the plan God had for her. He informed Mary that she would conceive a child in her womb and would deliver a son. He gave her his name—Jesus! As Gabriel presented to Mary the message from heaven, she was told that Jesus will be great and would be called the Son of God. He will be given the throne of David. He will reign forever and His kingdom shall never end! Mary did not doubt the word from heaven, but she did wonder how it would happen because she was not married. The angel told her that the Holy Ghost would come upon her and the power of God would overshadow her. The seed of God, the life of God Himself would be planted in her womb. Gabriel speaks clearly and directly to Mary as he says, "The holy and pure one that is born from you will be called the Son of God!" He also informed her that her cousin Elizabeth, who had no children and was well beyond child-bearing years, was in the sixth month of her pregnancy. Gabriel finished by saying, "For with God, nothing shall be impossible!"

A dual view opens in the hologram of heaven. We watch two scenes at once. The decision Mary would make will affect heaven and earth for all time. All the angels of heaven watch for Mary's response. Legions upon legions of angels, peer from the portals of glory—waiting. The Father knows from ages past what her response will be. He knows her heart of faith and her love for God. With love and favor, the Father is smiling upon the young woman called Mary, as she opens her life fully to God's purpose and plan. As all heaven is watching her on earth in one view of the hologram, in the corresponding view of earth as on the split screen, Gabriel awaits her response. We now see Mary as she says, "Behold, I am the servant of the Lord. Let it be done to me exactly as the word you have declared!"

Heaven rings with shouts of praise! We rejoice with the saints of all ages. From his throne at the right hand of the Father, Jesus, the Son of God, shares how that very night the presence of the Father, the anointing of the Holy Spirit, and the Son of God Himself enter the room where Mary slept. The Son of God declares that he laid aside His glory and heavenly power by choice and in the form of a seed, entered the womb of Mary. The seed was the Word spoken directly to Mary. When she received the Word by faith and spoke its truth into reality with her mouth, the miracle began! The life of Almighty God in seed form was now developing within the womb of Mary. The Son of God adds that God's words are spirit and they are life. *Every word of God is invested with the potential and impregnated with the power to produce what it proclaims!* These seeds sprout and spring forth with life when received and planted into the heart of a believing woman or man.

Because of the unique circumstances in which Jesus would be born by a virgin, it was necessary to prepare the heart of her betrothed as well. We see that the angel of the Lord appeared to Joseph in a dream, informing him that the child conceived within Mary's womb was of the Holy Ghost. He was instructed to have no fear, to take Mary as his wife, but to have no physical relationship with her until after the child was born. He was told to name the child Jesus because he would save his people from their sins.

The scene displayed within the hologram of heaven changes to nine months later. Mary, who is ready to deliver her child, has traveled with Joseph to Bethlehem because of a special tax imposed upon Israel by the Romans. Each man had to return to their native city for the census and to pay the tax bill. Even though Mary was pregnant, they still were required to obey. For nine months, the life of Jesus developed within her womb, and the time and place of His arrival had been foretold. It was a starlit night, a holy, heaven-sent night. The universe that the word of God created awaited in wonder for His humble arrival. The heavens that declared His glory sent a unique star to welcome him there. Angels from heaven could not be silent. They were amazed at the love God was displaying for man. In the hologram, a scan of the entire earth and its citizens on this night shows that all things seem as they always have been. Most men are totally unaware of the momentous, history changing event happening in Bethlehem. Most men did not even notice. He was born in a lowly stable. However, all the universe sang his praises as the angelic choir spilled out of heaven's portals rejoicing with the Father above. Shepherds on a hillside heard the angel choir singing. They were told of the Savior's birth. The lowly shepherds left their flocks to find where he lay and to worship the newborn king. Wise men recognized the signs in the heavens. They too came to worship the Savior, presenting gifts to the King of all kings. *A new species of man was birthed in the stable that night.* To the outside world, he was just another baby, but *a dynamic, seismic shift had just commenced.*

24

Covenant Life

A perfect life...

In the presence of our heavenly Father, listening to the Son of God during our imaginary excursion we are also praising the Lord for this glorious vision. God became man, what a miracle of grace! As *Story Time in Heaven* continues, we lean forward in anticipation, not wanting to miss a single thing!

The hologram before our eyes shows scenes of his development for the first thirty years. Nothing seems too unusual, just the normal growth and development of a young man—except for a trip to Jerusalem one year. The Son of God relates that as a man, He limited Himself to learning about his calling and his role. At an early age, he was aware his Father was God in heaven, not Joseph in the carpenter shop. He studied the Scriptures diligently and knew them better than any man. *For he was not just a man, He was God within man! He was not partially God and partially man; He is one hundred percent God and one hundred percent man!* Joseph heard this truth in a dream as well long before Jesus' birth. In this dream, he was informed by an angel of a prophecy spoken many years before by a prophet that a virgin would conceive a child who *would be called Emmanuel. This name means "God with us."*

The scene that caught our attention now appears in more detail on the hologram before us. At the age of twelve during one of the annual pilgrimages to Jerusalem, a journey his family would embark on each year for worship, Jesus sat down with the religious leaders. They were in the temple area, discussing the meaning and truths of scripture. Jesus was visiting with these respected theologians of the day, men who were supposed to *know* the depths and truths of the Scriptures well. We view this scene in the hologram of heaven and it makes us smile at their amazement. Jesus, at twelve years of age, is revealing incredible wisdom and insight with his questions and answers as they discuss the Scriptures together. We chuckle as we realize how little these leaders know. They do not know they are discussing the word of God with the very author who wrote them. No one knows Scripture as fully as Jesus. They have never heard anyone speak with such insight. Many rabbis ponder and take note of this young man from Galilee. Jesus was so engrossed in conversation and so trusted by his parents, that Mary and Joseph had already left for home assuming he was traveling with the family. When he could not be found, they turned back to Jerusalem looking for him. It was three days later when they finally tracked him down! Though the time for his ministry had not yet arrived, he already knew his Father's business was not carpentry but the salvation of lost souls. For many more years following this, the Son of God remained in Nazareth, learning and working in the carpenter's trade but always in communion with his Father in heaven.

The scene changes again. Jesus now appears to be thirty years of age. He is moving into the ministry and purpose for which he had come from heaven to earth. The Father informs us that His Son lived a perfect life. Jesus had never sinned, in thought, in word, or in deed. He did not have the penchant or the tendency to sin. When Adam was created in the garden, he did not have that tendency to sin either; but he disobeyed by choice. Adam was given the authority of sonship and dominion on earth in the garden of Eden but he failed miserably. He sinned by disobeying the Father's command. Unfortunately, this tendency to sin was passed on to all his descendants. Jesus was not born of Adam, he was born of the Almighty God! He was born in the authority of sonship and with the dominion that Adam had been given in the garden of Eden. The Father of love continues instructing us that with Jesus, He was starting fresh, a new beginning, a second chance for mankind.

The only desire and purpose of Jesus, the Son of God, was to be obedient to the will of His Father. His initial purpose was to succeed in the test over temptation in every area where Adam had failed. To prepare for the tests ahead, the scene shifts to the banks of the Jordan River as Jesus visits John the Baptist, the miracle child of Mary's cousin Elizabeth, born to her in her old age. John is calling people to repentance, instructing them to turn from their sins. He calls all who repent to be baptized in the Jordan River. We see him baptizing many who repented at his call. Jesus came to John to be baptized as well. But John, knowing in his heart that Jesus was the Messiah, resisted. He desired to reverse the roles and to be baptized by Jesus. This baptism of Jesus, the Son of God is directed by His Father to help fulfill His purpose. Acquiescing, John submitted to God's will by baptizing Jesus in the River Jordan just as Jesus requested. In this moment of public obedience and submission to the Father, we hear God speak a beautiful confirmation straight from heaven. The Father declares, "This is my beloved Son, in Him I am well pleased!" The Holy Spirit of God descends on Jesus from heaven and alights upon him like a dove. As we view this taking place, the Son of God in heaven's grandstand says, "At this point, I was anointed with the Spirit or God without measure. This preparation was needed for my ministry on the earth."

Following this, Jesus was led by the Spirit of God into a wilderness area. We see him there alone, praying and communicating with His heavenly Father. He is fasting, putting aside the flesh, focusing on the spirit, and strengthening Himself for the days ahead. After forty days and forty nights of fasting, He grew hungry. The tempter, the alien invader of this planet who deceived Eve in the garden, appeared. He endeavored to bring doubt to Jesus about His position as God's Son. He used the hunger in Jesus' flesh to tempt Him to prove He was the Son of God. The deceiver said, "*If You are the Son of God*, command that these stones be made bread." Jesus answered with the word. That is always the best response. He said, "It is written, 'Man shall not live by bread alone, but by every word that proceeds from the mouth of God.'" We see the tempter take Jesus to the city of Jerusalem and place him upon the pinnacle of the temple. There he tries to cause Jesus to doubt his sonship again. He says, "*If you are the Son of God*, cast yourself down: for it is written, 'He shall give his angel charge of you, and they will pick you up in their hands to keep you from even dashing your foot against a stone.' "The deceiver failed a second time, as Jesus answered with the word, "It is written again, 'You, shall not tempt the Lord your God.' "The hologram takes us with Jesus and the tempter to a very high mountain. There he shows the Son of God all the kingdoms of the world and the glory of them. He then says to Jesus, "All these things will I give You if You fall down and worship me." We see Jesus rebuke the tempter by saying, "Get away from here, Satan! It is written, 'You shall worship the Lord your God, and Him only shall you serve.'"

How glorious is this vision? Where Adam had failed, Jesus succeeded! We now see angels from heaven coming to minister to Jesus. The Son of God has stood firm against the alien invader! In the power of the spirit and in the knowledge of his sonship, Jesus the Messiah spent three years establishing God's kingdom back on the earth.

Viewing this in the hologram of heaven, we observe amazing and miraculous sights. Traveling all throughout the area, Jesus teaches the word, refuting the lies of the deceiver. He journeys from town to town, sharing the love of his Father. Multitudes are sick, multitudes are suffering the effects of the alien invader's hold. Jesus is healing them all. Sickness is part of the curse. But Jesus is not under the curse, He is walking in the power of God. His authority is so powerful that as a storm rages and those who were traveling with Him were gripped with fear, Jesus used His delegated authority and commanded the storm to end. He simply said, "Peace, be still!" In heaven's grandstand, the saints of all ages are clapping their hands and shouting for joy as miracle upon miracle is displayed. Satan's power is being crushed by our Lord. We see blind eyes opened, deaf ears hear, the lame can walk, the unclean outcasts with the contagious disease of leprosy are returned to their family and homes completely healed! When His disciples had fished in vain, He simply told them to cast their nets on the other side of the boat. A command in the spirit no one heard but the fish, drove them right into the awaiting nets. His authority and dominion included the fish of the sea, the fowl of the air, and everything that moved on the earth. He had authority over the winds and the waves and the sea. The trees obeyed him. In fact, when He cursed a fig tree for not producing fruit, it dried up from the roots within one day! He told His disciples that this power was available to them as well. They could command mountains to move, if need be!

Jesus as the second Adam is exercising power and authority the way Adam did not, He is putting such a powerful stop to the invader's hold upon mankind that he even raises the dead! The standing ovations in heaven around us are incredible! Shouts of "Hallelujah! Praise the Lord! Glory to God!" rise amid the drum rolls and cymbals, as in heaven, we behold this wondrous life! Any soul who reached out in faith, believing his words, were blessed with the answer to their prayers. Jesus fed thousands with next to nothing. He had the power to bless and multiply so the supply would always meet the need. I now understand even more clearly how the Apostle John could write, "And the Word was made flesh, and dwelt among us, (and we beheld his glory, the glory as of the only begotten of the Father,) full of grace and truth" (Jn. 1:14, KJV).

We watch Jesus as He calls and trains His disciples, and we all hear the parables and wisdom that He shares. In his teaching, he declares truths of the kingdom of heaven and describes the glory of the Father's love. His Father is the Good Shepherd looking for His lost sheep. He is also the Father in heaven who watches for the return of His wandering, wayward son. There is joy, laughter, and tenderness evidenced in the disciples' relationship with the Son of God.

For three years, our Savior shows us, the power
of a life lived in obedience to God.

He models the life that man was designed to live. He displays the character of God. We observe Him saying to His disciples, "If you have seen me, you have seen my Father!" Some of the stories, we are seeing in the hologram of heaven we have never seen before!

180

However, the Apostle John told us clearly, "And there are also many other things which Jesus did, the which, if they should be written every, one; I suppose that even the world itself could not contain the books that should be written. Amen" (Jn. 21:25, KJV).

Often early in the morning or late in the evening, we see Jesus slip away to a quiet place alone. There He communes with His heavenly Father. He receives direction and strength for each day. There is much ahead that our Savior will face. Toward the end of these three years, packed with power and glory and grace, we sense a change beginning to take place. This earthly period of ministry, we are told by the Father was to allow His son Jesus to set an example and create a true picture of what the Father desires for all His children. We are being given a pattern for every man, to follow in faith. Ahead is now a purpose only the Messiah Jesus Christ can accomplish.

As we are viewing, in the hologram of heaven, suddenly we have a split-screen view. We have four scenes before us at once! We sense an awe as if everyone in heaven's grandstand is catching their breath, impressed and awestruck by this multiple panoramic view. Each scene is occurring at the very, same moment in time. One view takes us to heaven where the Father of love and the angelic hosts alone are seen. There are no citizens in heaven, the mansions are empty, and the golden streets quiet as none have yet arrived! The second screen or unique view in the hologram, (not quite sure, in earth's terms, how this multiple and magnificent viewing can be described) is of Christ on earth, and all that he is experiencing. The third area within the hologram is a live view—or so it seems of all the saints of ages past, waiting in paradise and longing for their eternal home! However, something is very puzzling about the fourth dimension, it is somehow, blocked or blurred from our view.

We are instructed by the Father to witness, to watch, and observe closely, to pay attention to what the work of Christ, the Son of God, is doing on earth. This work will influence dynamic change in every dimension at the very same time. *All of heaven, all of earth, and all of eternity shall forever be impacted by the force of this one, solitary life.* Three dimensions in our view are in unison, anticipating victory and amazing blessings as a result. The fourth dimension in the hologram, which is hidden from our view, we sense is of the opponent's plans for defeating God's Son. To assist and strengthen Jesus for the climax of the ages, individuals from each of the three dimensions we can view send representatives to encourage him. The fourth dimension, we sense, sends others to thwart God's magnificent plan.

On earth, the Spirit guides as Jesus leads his inner circle high into a mountain apart from others. There with Peter, James, and John, his closest friends and disciples, on earth; we witness the merging of three dimensions. Appearing before them, we see Moses, the giver of the law, and Elijah, the great prophet of Israel!! They have come from paradise at the Father's request. The Son of God, Jesus Christ, is transfigured before them. The glory of God within him—clothed in human flesh to all others—is released for us to see. Our hearts burn, our spirits soar at the sight of the one who is both God and man! The face of Jesus shines with the brilliance of the sun. His clothing, the robe of glory, is as brilliant and white as light! We are seeing before us the fully developed revelation of the Son who is both God and man! The seed of God's Word planted in Mary's womb over thirty years before, now appears in his fullness before our eyes! He *will* fulfill completely the law of Moses and fulfill every messianic prophecy, that has been made!

Observing the Son of God in His meeting with Moses and Elijah, the disciples are amazed! We smile as Peter says, "This is a great place to be. If you want, we can build a tabernacle here for each of you, Jesus, Moses, and Elijah!" No one answered his question because at that very moment, the Shekinah glory of God from Heaven; overshadowed them. The Father of Love, spoke clearly in confirmation, approval, and love. He said, "This is my beloved Son, in whom I am well pleased. Listen to him."

From the Glory of heaven's portals to the dimension of paradise, to earth's mountain of transfiguration, all three dimensions are joined together with one purpose. The course is set for the greatest action ever accomplished by God's amazing grace!

25

Covenant Sacrifice

A perfect sacrifice . . .

For a moment, the multiscreen hologram dissolves. We are in the throne room of God, the core of eternity; the power center for all that has been or ever shall be; and the source of all life, all light, and all power forever! In our imagination, we have tapped into the story of the ages. We are in the presence of the Father of love, the glorious Son of God, and the dynamic Holy Spirit. The Triune God, who fills all things, manifests His glory in this place like no other. Multitudes of angels are attending Him, saints from all ages past worship Him, and we are in awe of His glory.

Before continuing with the story, we must pause to acknowledge and glorify the Father of love and His glorious Son. We open our hearts to His truth as we approach the day above all days. Before us today, we know is the pivotal day, the most significant day in the history of the entire universe. With great anticipation, the entire family of God concentrates our focus upon the magnificent screen of the hologram before us. Its magnetic pull draws us in as *Story Time in Heaven* continues. Only one scene, one view appears initially. We are drawn into a large upper-level room. The room contains a long banquet table with candlesticks upon it for light. It is early evening as a dozen men are reclining around this table with Jesus. They are his disciples. We see Peter, James, and John, the men who were on the mount of transfiguration with Jesus in our last scene. This is a meeting and a meal like none other!

As we are entering in to the experience in the upper room, the Son of God, on His throne in heaven, is describing what is happening before our eyes. He describes first His awareness in that moment on earth. He had the knowledge that the Father of love had given everything into His hands. He was fully aware that He came from God and that He was preparing to go back to God. *Though born as a man, He had no doubts about His position, His power, or His purpose.* In full knowledge of this, He rose from the table, took off His cloak, wrapped a servant's towel around His waist, and began washing His disciples' feet. He washed the feet of those who would soon flee in His hour of need, the one who would deny that he even knew Jesus three times, and even the one who would betray Him that night! *What an amazing act of love and grace!* Shortly after this, Judas knowing his betrayal had been exposed, fled.

In this hour, Jesus instituted a new blood covenant. From this day forward, no one would ever have the need to sacrifice a lamb or a goat or a bull to cover their sins and be blessed by God. From this point forward, because of what Jesus the Messiah would accomplish in a few short hours, all would change. Adam had been plunged into sin and death by doubt and disobedience. Jesus, the second Adam, will create a new species of man by faith, obedience, and sacrifice. It will forever be remembered and commemorated by the simple act of communion. Jesus took bread, broke it and then he said, "This is my body, broken for you." Then He also gave them the cup, saying, "This is my blood of the new covenant." As often as we eat this bread and drink this cup, we show the power of His death until He returns. As they sat around the table, Jesus informs His disciples that all will change after this night. He is leaving. He will die and go back to His Father. His disciples become very troubled by what Jesus is saying, but we hear the comforting word of Jesus to his confused and troubled disciples. "Let not your hearts be troubled. You believe in God, believe also in me. In my Father's house are many mansions. If it were not so, I would have told you. I am going to prepare a place for you. I will come back again and take you with me to where I am." He also adds, "I am the way, the truth, and the life. No man comes to the Father but by me." He then prayed a prayer to His Father for His disciples; in fact, for everyone who would follow Him in the generations to come. Many other truths were shared that night around the table. They ended by singing a hymn together then proceeded to the garden of Gethsemane. In the garden, He prayed, interceded, and prepared for the onslaught ahead. He then bowed to His Father's will. He was betrayed, abandoned, denied. He was lied about, abused, and despised. He was unjustly tried and condemned to die!

The religious leaders asked him, "Are you the Christ? Are you God's Son?" When He acknowledged that he was, they called him a heretic. Pilate, earth's judge, asked him, "Are you the King of the Jews?" Everyone wants to know, "Who is He?" The tempter from the garden of Eden was frantic! He wanted Jesus to deny His true place. He tried so hard in the wilderness to promote doubt about the fact He was God's son Why? All through His journey and ministry, people wondered about Jesus. No one had ever talked like Him with such authority and love. No one had ever done the miracles he had done. No one had ever commanded the winds, the waves, and the sea. *Who is he? That is what everyone wants to know!*

In the hologram before us, the scenes of his final hours play frame after frame for our view. Though I have read the story over and over through the years of my life, to see it visualized before us and experience the story this way as though we were there magnifies the power of its impact on our lives. Our hearts ache as tears fill our eyes! The citizens of heaven are aghast at the display of pain and shame that He bears. The earth itself shakes and trembles in the awareness that the weight of sin for every man for all time has been placed upon Jesus! The tortuous contortions of sickness and pain flow into His body. The penalty for all men's evil is upon Him. In the throes of death's grip and in great pain; *the Son of God, never forgot who He was.* Of the mockers and tormentors around Him, He said, "Father, forgive them for they know not what they do." To a condemned but repentant sinner, hanging on a cross beside him, He spoke, "This day, you will be with me in paradise!" as the sinner reached out to him in faith. The torment and pressure of man's sin and its penalties grew more intense with each passing moment. The sun refuses to shine on this scene. Dark clouds roll in and thunder peels! His body is so marred and wracked with pain that He is unrecognizable! In the darkness, He cries out in sorrow, "My God! My God! Why have You forsaken Me?" He experiences for all men the separation from the Father of love. At the end of his suffering and excruciating pain when the final payment for sin had been paid; He spoke these three simple, words, "*It is finished!*" Then into the Father's hands, He released His spirit.

At the exact moment of his death, the split-screens appear in the hologram of heaven. In one image, we see the shock of priests at the temple in Jerusalem. Before their eyes, the veil separating the holy of holies from the holy place is torn in two from top to bottom as if by the hand of God! In another scene within the hologram, we see the Son of God arrive in the divided area of paradise! Initially, He arrives on the side of the tormented spirits, journeying there for fallen man. However, it could not contain, the purity and power of the Son of God. He removed the keys of death, hell, and the grave from the alien invader's hand. He is that old serpent, the devil. Jesus, the Son of God, then did what no other had ever done. By the power of his purity and sacrifice and by his power and dominion as God's Son. He crossed the gulf to the other side and entered paradise!

The next view in the hologram shows the heavenly throne room that day! Angels cried, "Holy, holy is the Lord!" They are amazed at the demonstration of power and love, displayed by the Son of God. The Father of love proclaims to the angels around, "My Son and our family will soon arrive! Prepare for His return! The Father awaits His only begotten Son! The Father awaits the souls in paradise. The Father awaits the citizens of heaven and their arrival. Their mansions await them as well. The Father awaits His family! In the scene near the cross, the earth shook, rocks split open, and tombs opened. Many dead saints will appear after His resurrection to testify of His sacrifice. A hardened Roman Centurion, who had witnessed much death, was overcome by the display of pain and horror exacted upon Jesus. He was filled with awe and fear by the earthquake and all that happened around the moment of His death. In astonishment of the scene around him, the Centurion said, "Truly, this was the son of God!" Disciples mourned. Those who loved him cried, it appears to the world around that God has died. A hush of mourning, a quiet grief, and a deep, sinking, feeling of eternal loss penetrates earth's atmosphere. The Creator of the world had been rejected by the world. He came to His own, but they neither recognized nor received Him. *Most thought he was a mere man.*

The hologram of heaven in our imagination now shows us beneath the surface in other realms. There is so much more for the eye to see! In paradise, saints of all ages past are hearing from the Son of God. There are multitudes, millions of souls are present. We see Moses and Elijah; Abraham, Isaac, and Jacob; and Joseph and King David. A great host of departed souls, who died in faith, from all ages past! They are the ones who, by faith and the covenant sacrifice, followed God in their lives on the earth. Jesus is preaching to them, showing himself to be the sacrifice for their sins. As they hear and believe, paradise pulsates with praise. We see these saints begin to understand *that sacrifices made in the past only covered their sins.* Jesus Christ shares that *His blood will cleanse their sin for all eternity!!* Everyone in paradise embraces the truth and worships the Son of God!

For three days, earth seems silent, brooding..., and waiting answers.
Paradise awaits in expectation and desire.
Heaven awaits the arrival of its own.

26

We've Only Just Begun

The third day arrives…

On earth, there is a cleanness, a freshness, a new day of hope arising. Something feels unusually, different from the night that has passed.

In the spirit of our imagination, we hear the voice of the Father who calls to His Son as He sends the Spirit of God in great power to reunite Jesus with His body of flesh. However, this body is not like the one He laid down. This new body is prepared to live in heaven, transformed in new creation power and eternal life. The Spirit of God in mighty and dynamic power, unites the eternal Son of God with his body as a man in eternal, resurrection power. Jesus is the first fruits of the resurrection. He is a brand-new species of being, a new creation. Angel armies escort the Son into the presence of the Father as he places his sacrificial blood on the mercy seat of heaven. His blood will forever flow over the golden covenant container before the presence of the Father's throne. This scarlet liquid flows with unending, divine, power. The blood of Christ has, for man, paid the penalty for his sin and opened the way, to the very presence of God! Jesus, the Son of God, is raised from the dead and now seated in the Father's right hand in heavenly places. He is far above all rule and authority and power and dominion. His name is above all names in title and authority and power for all eternity! The Father declares that He has put all things under the feet of Jesus Christ. It is now time for the Son, to make His resurrection known to his disciples. He must also, bring the saints of all ages, waiting in paradise to their mansions prepared in heaven.

We are viewing from the portals of heaven on the amazing split-screen three-dimensional hologram all three realms at once—heaven, the earth, and paradise. As they relive the glorious resurrection morning, many in heaven's grandstand are cheering, shouting, and praising God! They are the ones, who were in paradise on that resurrection morning! They are rejoicing in the story, remembering the glorious journey to heaven. Jesus Christ, the resurrected Son of God with multitudes of angels is ushering them to their heavenly mansions. As they walked out to the city called heaven, we see the wonderful speakers we heard during *Story Time in Heaven*. We see Noah, Moses, and Joseph. There are many more stories we would love to hear when we return on a future imaginary journey. Those who are filling the celestial city with their presence are not in resurrected bodies like Christ. They are in heaven only in their souls and their spirits. We all are told that another day is coming when they will have a body like the risen Christ. All of creation groans and longs for that day, for the full manifestation of the sons of God! I want to learn more about that day, but we sense this first imaginary excursion will be ending soon. Paradise is now empty. However, the other side of the gulf in that dimension is filled with millions of departed souls, which was constantly growing in number. I wonder about them and what is ahead for this group of souls.

At the tomb in the garden where the body of Jesus was laid, wonder and confusion prevailed as Jesus' body is missing! Initially, powerful angels appeared outside the sealed tomb. Soldiers, guarding the tomb fled at the angel sighting. Easily, the stone was rolled away. Remaining there for a while, they revealed to the world, "Christ is risen! Why are you seeking Him among the dead?" Appearing in His glorified body, not bound by earthly constraints, Jesus appeared often, beginning that resurrection day. He made his presence known in different locations. Jerusalem in the upper room or outside the garden tomb. He was seen on the road to Emmaus and by the Sea of Galilee. He showed himself individually to some, but often in groups of gathered disciples. He walked with two disciples as they traveled to Emmaus. These two were leaving Jerusalem, troubled by all that they had heard. Jesus walked with them, talked with them and guided the conversation to help them understand that it was necessary for the savior to die for man's sin. They did not recognize him as Jesus because of their sorrow, until he sat with them and broke bread and blessed it at their meal. Beholding his nail pierced hands, they believed! On one occasion, he visibly appeared, to more than five hundred at one time. For a period of forty days, he met, encouraged, and instructed his disciples. He showed himself alive to them by many infallible proofs! He released the breath of God, the new creation life, into their souls. They were born of the spirit! Their doubts were gone...

On the last day, before leaving, Jesus continued to open the Scriptures to their understanding. He instructed them that it was necessary that He leave. He will request the Father to send the Holy Spirit of God in His place. He will anoint them and lead them into all truth. As they walked out as far as Bethany, Jesus lifted his hands and blessed them. As he was departing from them, being carried into heaven, they heard him saying, "Lo, I am with you always, even unto the end of the world." As they stood gazing upward, angels asked them a question, "Why are you gazing into heaven. This same Jesus shall come back again as you've seen him go!" They *knew* He truly is the Son of God!

In our imagination we are now back in the Throne Room of heaven. All other scenes and images on the screens before us have dissolved. We are viewing the grandstand of heaven filled with the millions of rejoicing saints as together we all bask in the presence of the Father of Love and His glorious Son, seated at His right hand. This is where Story Time in Heaven began, but, we sense our first imaginary journey to heaven is ending. We perceive a change in our ability to focus on the scene in heaven's grandstand as we appear to be drifting away. We feel ourselves becoming aware of our movement out of heaven and across the reaches of eternity. We fight it, longing to remain and learn more. However, we are powerless to resist, unable to keep ourselves from slipping away from this amazing adventure. We are tumbling, cascading, falling from the eternal realm back into the confines of space and time. We move through the billions of galaxies in dizzying speed, moving past stars and planetary systems into our own Milky Way finally entering back into earth's domain and moving into our bodies, slipping back into an earth suit of flesh just like a hand re-entering a glove.

We find ourselves here—in this moment—with a book called Story Time in Heaven in our hands. We are back where we first began our imaginary journey and at that place where we had been curiously wondering what it would be like to embark on an excursion to heaven. Since then we have imagined and seen so much! Yet, we long to return some day and learn more. In fact, we desire to make heaven our home someday, not just in our imagination but in reality! When we finish our lives here on earth, we desire to join the citizens of Heaven whose lives we witnessed in the Celestial City during our imaginary travels. We ponder what we learned, what we saw and what we experienced of God and His Love! For a moment we close our eyes in meditation and remembrance. In our imagination a window into heaven opens. The curtain is pulled back and we see the glorious Son of God on his throne, His eyes looking directly into our own. He speaks to us with great love as He asks a question, "Don't you see how real this is?" Somehow, we know and acknowledge that this adventure was far more than imagination! Heaven we recognize and affirm is a real place! Jesus then asks another question that we somehow know will affect our lives for the rest of time and for all eternity. Many throughout the ages, have had a variety of answers to this question. Only one answer is true. Jesus had asked the same question He is asking us now to one of His disciples, Peter. He said, "Who do you say that I am?" Peter's response was, "You are the Christ, the Son of the living God!" This realization is foundational to all truth. Accepting, believing and confessing or acknowledging this fact—settles our destiny!

Now from the windows of heaven, Jesus is looking at each of us. He is peering from the Throne Room in heaven, gazing intently into the room where we are this very moment and seeing into our hearts as He is asking sincerely, "Who do YOU say that I am?"

"He was in the world, and the world was made by him, and the world knew him not. He came unto his own, and his own received him not. But as many as received him, to them gave he the power to become the sons of God, even to them that believe on his name." (John 1:10-12, KJV)

Study Notes

Chapter 1

1. John 14:2–3
2. Revelation 4:1 to 5:14
3. Revelation 21:1 to 22:5
4. Matthew 6:19–21

Chapter 2

1. Ephesians 2:7
2. Nicene Creed
3. Apostles Creed
4. Athanasian Creed
5. Genesis 1:1 to 2:5
6. The Institute for Creation Research – Recent Creation Confirmed Podcast by Brian Thomas, M.S. www.icr.org
7. John 1:1–3
8. Psalm 19:1–4; Psalm 33:6–9
9. Isaiah 45:18
10. Acts 17:24–28
11. Romans 1:10–22
12. Hebrews 11:3
13. The Institute for Creation Research – The Heavens Declare – www.icr.org/creation-galaxies
14. https://youtu.be/jfSNxVqprvM – Eye to the Universe
15. Nehemiah 9:6

Chapter 3

1. Genesis 2:6–25
2. Psalm 8:4–9
3. Psalm 139:14
4. Job 33:4
5. Psalm 100:3

Chapter 4 & 5

    1.   Genesis 3:1–24

Chapter 6

    1.   Genesis 4:1 to 9:17
    2.   Hebrews 11:4, 7
    3.   Institute for Creation Research – Dinosaur Tracks Back Noah's Flood – Brian Thomas M.S., and Tim Clarey, Ph.D. www.icr.org
    4.   Institute for Creation Research – Embracing Catastrophic Plate Tectonics – Tim Clarey, Ph.D. www.icr.org

Chapter 8

    1.   Genesis 11:1 to 18:15
    2.   Hebrews 11:17–19

Chapter 9

    1.   Genesis 21:1 to 22:18
    2.   Hebrews 11:17–19

Chapter 10

    1.   Genesis 37:1–36
    2.   Genesis 39: 1–6

Chapter 11

    1.   Genesis 39:7 to 41:44
    2.   2 Corinthians 1:20 Amplified Version

Chapter 12

    1.   Genesis 41:45 to 47:11
    2.   Genesis 11:6
    3.   Proverbs 18:21

Chapter 13

    1.   Revelation 20:11–15
    2.   Matthew 25:41
    3.   Revelation 21:10–27

Chapter 14

 1. Exodus 1:1 to 15:21

Chapter 15

 1. Hebrews 11:23–29
 2. Exodus 24:1–18
 3. Exodus 25:1 to 40:38
 4. Deuteronomy 27:1 to 28:13
 5. Deuteronomy 30:19
 6. Numbers 13:1 to 14:9

Chapter 16

 1. Psalm 23

Chapter 17

 1. Psalm 8:1,3–4
 2. Psalm 103:13–14
 3. Psalm 103:1–3
 4. 1 Samuel 16:1 to 17:58
 5. Numbers 13:1 to 14:9
 6. Hebrews 3:8–19
 7. Hebrews 4:1–2

Chapter 18

 1. 2 Samuel 9:1–13
 2. 1 Samuel 18:1–5
 3. 1 Samuel 20:1–42
 4. 1 Samuel 19:9–18a

Chapter 19 & 20

 1. 1 Kings 3:3–14
 2. 2 Chronicles 1:1 to 9:31
 3. Proverbs 15:4
 4. Proverbs 18:20–21

Chapter 21

1. 1 Kings 11:1–43
2. Ecclesiastes 1:17–18
3. Ecclesiastes 2:1–18
4. Ecclesiastes 12:1–2
5. Ecclesiastes 12:13–14
6. Luke 15:11–32
7. Psalm 84:1
8. Psalm 139:1–18
9. Luke 16:19–31

Chapter 22

1. 2 Corinthians 5:6–8
2. Hebrews 1:3
3. Psalm 138:2
4. Acts 17:23–28
5. Hebrews 9:22
6. Leviticus 17:14
7. 2 Chronicles 16:9
8. 2 Peter 3:9
9. Galatians 3:23–28
10. Luke 16:19–31
11. Matthew 24:35

Chapter 23

1. Luke 1:1 to 2:20
2. Hebrews 4:12
3. Matthew 1:18–25
4. Matthew 2:1–11

Chapter 24

1. Matthew 1:23
2. Luke 2:40–52
3. Matthew 3:1–17
4. Matthew 4:1–11
5. John 1:14
6. John 21:25
7. Matthew 17:1–6
8. Mark 9:2–8

Chapter 25

1. John 13:1–30
2. Luke 22:17–20
3. Matthew 26:26–30
4. 1 Corinthians 11:23–26
5. John 14:1–6
6. John 17:1–26
7. Luke 22:39–44
8. Luke 23:34
9. Luke 23:43
10. Matthew 27:54

Chapter 26

1. Matthew 28:1–20
2. Mark 16:1–20
3. Luke 24:1–53
4. John 20:1 to 21:25
5. Acts 1:1–11
6. Matthew 16:13–18
7. John 1:10–12

About the Author

Born and raised in a pastor's home in Canada, G. T. Froese was taught from his earliest days about the truths of God's word and the reality of heaven. Throughout his life, he has lived in both Canada and the USA and has been an avid student of God's Word. He traveled verse by verse through the entire Bible each year for many years. Over time, he worked in a variety of fields. He traveled to Israel, Europe, and to over thirty countries. He also served as a pastor and a teacher. G. T. Froese now resides in Florida with his wife and closest friend, Brenda.

CPSIA information can be obtained
at www.ICGtesting.com
Printed in the USA
BVHW082015070119
537251BV00007B/135/P